Just One Look

The Billionaire Barons of Texas · Book Twelve

CHRIS KENISTON

Indie House Publishing

Indie House Publishing

MORE BOOKS
By Chris Keniston

The Billionaire Barons of Texas
Just One Date
Just One Spark
Just One Dance
Just One Take
Just One Taste
Just One Shot
Just One Chance
Just One Mistake
Just One Family
Just One Rodeo
Just One Surprise
Just One Look

Hart Land
Heather
Lily
Violet
Iris
Hyacinth
Rose
Calytrix
Zinnia
Poppy
Picture Perfect

Farraday Country
Adam
Brooks
Connor
Declan
Ethan

Finn
Grace
Hannah
Ian
Jamison
Keeping Eileen
Loving Chloe
Morgan
Neil
Owen
Paxton
Quinn

Honeymoon Series
Honeymoon for One
Honeymoon for Three
Honeymoon for Four
Honeymoon for Five
Honeymoon for Six
Honeymoon for Seven

Aloha Romance Series:
Aloha Texas
Almost Paradise
Mai Tai Marriage
Dive Into You
Look of Love
Love by Design
Love Walks In
Shell Game
Flirting with Paradise

Surf's Up Flirts:
(Aloha Series Companions)
Shall We Dance
Love on Tap
Head Over Heels
Perfect Match
Just One Kiss
It Had to Be You
Cat's Meow

CHAPTER ONE

"Someone pass the potatoes, please." Devlin Baron had no idea why not a single of the finest restaurants in the world could make garlic mashed potatoes the way Hazel, the family cook, did. If he could have only one food for the rest of his life, it would be a tough choice between any pasta dish in Hazel's homemade marinara sauce or her garlic mashed potatoes. Thankfully, he didn't need to choose.

"The way you shovel those potatoes down," his cousin Eve shook her head, "I don't understand why you aren't as wide as you are tall."

"Good metabolism." Devlin grinned back at his cousin.

"Good genetics don't hurt either." His sister Leah waved a fork at her cousin.

What didn't hurt was working out every morning without fail. On Devlin's thirtieth birthday, he realized if he didn't want to increase his pant size every year and still enjoy good food, he'd have to make some serious changes in his routine, and burning calories with an early morning workout had done the trick.

"All I have to say," his other cousin Paige frowned at him, "is the charity gala is in just a week and you'd better still fit in your tux."

"My tux fits just fine." Though maybe if he'd just put on a few pounds instead of keeping fit, his cousin would stop roping him into the blasted bachelor auction. Nothing was more degrading than having rich, bored women bid on a person as if they were Lamborghini seized by the DEA.

"You don't need to sound so grumpy about it." Paige's gaze lingered on him. "It's for a very worthy cause."

Which was the only reason he did this at all. Even though every year for the last five years his good friend and favorite plus one Emily had been buying him, adding to the gossip mill that they had a thing going. What no one knew was that the funds came from Devlin's bank account every auction. Especially since every year that Courtney Collins Baker Rothschild, now Miller, and soon to be who knew who, disposed of her most recent husband, she would bid on Devlin with a vengeance. Two years ago Emily had a sneezing fit and Courtney almost won. Scared Devlin half to death. Courtney had been a barracuda when she'd set her sights on a Baron after divorcing her first husband. Only the appeal of the Rothschild name had distracted her from her mission of landing a Baron spouse. Now searching for hubby number four, Devlin knew the woman would be there with an open checkbook.

"Why is Devlin the only bachelor Baron?" Siobhan glanced at him before looking back to Paige.

"Only one Baron in an auction so we get a guarantee of top dollar. We really cleaned up the year Kyle stepped in for Devlin."

"Must have been the race car thing," Devlin teased.

"Ha ha." Kyle rolled his eyes at his cousin. "Thank heaven Courtney was on her honeymoon with Rothschild that year or I'd have been toast."

Leaning over the side of her chair, his grandmother Lila Baron scratched her dog Honey behind the ears. "I think it's wonderful that you do this every year for such a good cause."

His grandmother was right. That's why he coughed up five figures every year to beat out Courtney. There were several things that Devlin was a sucker for, children, animals, and the underdog were top of his list, and the annual gala benefiting children aging out of the foster care system hit two of the top three things that he thought mattered more than the money in his bank account.

About to serve himself one more spoonful of Hazel's beloved mashed potatoes, his phone dinged. Immediately his gaze shot up to meet his grandfather's. Phones were a major no-no at the Baron dinner table. Normally he had his on vibrate, but tonight he'd forgotten to shift it before sitting down. "Excuse me a moment."

Normally it would never occur to Devlin to leave the dinner table, but he'd been waiting to hear from his team on the newest project that was down to the wire. Devlin did commercial real estate development, but somehow he'd found himself dipping his toe into a residential project and now that the interest rates had risen higher than the noon sun, he was second-guessing his decision to take on this particular project. "Hello."

"Sorry to bother you during dinner." His right-hand man had worked for him long enough to know how important family dinner time was. "I found another source for staging. This one comes highly recommended and hopefully they'll live up to the hype."

Staging residential property in Houston wasn't as popular as other parts of the country and, of course, the number one company for the job had almost every stock item in use for the Annual Rodeo. Who knew that a family rodeo even would require so much staging furniture. "Great. How fast?"

"Not as fast as you'd like, but better than the alternative option. The main three models will be fully staged next Monday."

"I suppose that's better than a poke in the eye with a stick." Unlike most residential developments, this was a scattering of new and remodeled homes just north of the hustle and bustle of growing suburban communities. If they didn't get them up and ready for showing before the spring rush, they'd be beaten down by the competition. He didn't like it. But another week was better than the three-week timeline their regular staging company had provided. "I trust your judgment. Let's go for it."

Elizabeth Louise Carter had been looking forward to her

upcoming visit with her sister Emily. After much schmoozing and tooting her own horn, Liz was excited to be heading to Houston next week, combining business with pleasure.

"The drapery workroom is behind schedule." Liz's office manager rolled her eyes and sighed. "I wish they weren't so good at their job because they are the most unorganized operation I've ever seen."

"That's the price of artistry." Liz had to admit that Josephine Garcia knew how to make a statement with custom upholstery. For small home projects, artistry wasn't required, but for the larger challenges, she needed Josephine's vision.

"If you say so." Her assistant sighed and then snapped her fingers. "Oh, your sister called while you were on the phone with Mr. Belker."

"Thanks. I'll call her now." The Belker remodel was one job she deeply regretted taking on. Not that it was over her head, just breaking her heart. Mr. Belker was nice enough. A senior gentleman from family money and style had bought one of Dallas's oldest homes on Swiss Avenue. He'd also married a woman half his age with the taste of a garden snail and hired Liz to help his new bride decorate the venerable old home. The house probably knew more about Mrs. Belker than Liz had—the moment they'd stepped out of the car to walk through the property, Liz could have sworn she saw the stately manor cringe. An hour later as Mrs. Belker bounced through the house criticizing every inch of detailed trim work and ornate workmanship, Liz wanted to run and hide. When Mrs. Belker suggested they tear down the semicircle grand staircase in the foyer and replace it with a modern floating staircase with iron rope rails, it took every ounce of reserve not to barf on the original polished marble floors.

The thought of destroying all the carefully crafted and irreplaceable grandeur of the old home was enough to make Liz cry. The problem, of course, was that walking away from the job only meant that someone else would destroy the home. Instead, she'd been stalling while racking her brain on how to make the smitten old goat and his youthful trophy wife update the house into the new millennium without losing all its valuable charm. So far she was failing miserably.

"Hey, sis." The sound of Emily's voice was a welcome reprieve from Liz's crazy day.

"Hey," Liz responded.

"Ooh, that sounds ominous."

"How can 'hey' sound ominous?"

"It's not the word, it's the tone. I've been listening to yours for nine months longer than we've been alive. I know that tone. What's wrong?"

"Not wrong just… well, yes wrong. I think I'm on the wrong side of the generation gap."

"You're not old enough to be on the wrong side. And I should know because I know exactly how old you are."

One thing was true, if anyone could read her moods with just one word, it was Emily. "This new bride, barely old enough to legally drink, wants to destroy a beautiful old house and modernize it. And I use that word very, very loosely."

"How modern?"

Liz actually groaned, loudly.

"Oh dear."

"Yep. That about says it all. I've been doing my best to stall, but I'm running out of excuses."

"Stall?"

"I don't want to just walk away because some other unscrupulous designer will do whatever they want for the paycheck."

"Maybe you need to do just that. At least it won't be on your conscience."

"Of course it will." Liz sighed. "I wonder…"

"What? In case you've forgotten, we have the death penalty in Texas for premeditated murder."

Oh, how Liz loved her sister. The laugh was exactly what she needed. "I was thinking more if I'm in Houston, they'll just have to wait for the preliminary drawings."

"Will they?"

"Probably. They picked me after my remodel of the Dugan house made the cover of the *Dallas Magazine*. Since the child bride wants to brag that *I* redid her house, yeah, I think she'll wait. Besides, she's perfectly content throwing parties in the first Mrs. Belker's twenty thousand square foot mansion on Straight Lane."

"Maybe she'll get used to it and give up on the new one."

"That would be too easy." Liz glanced up at the calendar on her wall. "I know I'm not supposed to arrive for a few more days, but what say you to having your favorite sister—"

"And older."

"By seven lousy minutes."

"Whatever." She could hear her sister's amusement over the phone. Emily loved teasing Liz for being older.

"Okay. Your favorite, older, sister visiting for an extra weekend? Thought I'd pop into town tomorrow and we can have a wild Friday night eating popcorn and watching old movies."

"Yes to all but the popcorn and old movies. Friday is the big Baron Bachelor Auction. I have to be there."

"To bail Devlin out. Got it."

"You can come too. It's usually a fun event and the food is always amazing at the old country club."

"Actually," her spirits began to lift, "I bought a fabulous dress on sale months ago and am still looking for some place to wear it. Sounds like your little shindig is the ticket."

"Terrific. I'll get you a seat at our table."

"Done. Who knows, maybe I'll find myself a fun bachelor to bid on."

"Elizabeth Louise."

"Only kidding." Liz laughed loudly. *Maybe.*

CHAPTER TWO

Thanks to a handful of complications popping up at the last minute, Devlin and Emily had agreed to meet at the gala. Now here he was struggling with the stupid bow tie on his tux and watching the clock on the wall. He should just keep a stash of clip-on ties for nights like tonight when his fingers and the real bow tie did not want to cooperate.

His phone buzzing on the nightstand, Devlin growled at the stupid tie and resisted the urge to fling it aside as he answered the cell. "Yes."

"Oh, we're having a good night, are we?" Emily's voice was warm with amusement. "Let me guess. Your tie?"

"Always."

"Put it in your pocket. I'll help you with it when you get to the gala."

"Deal." Without a second thought, he shoved the tie into his pocket. "I'll be heading out the door any second now."

"I just wanted to let you know I'm running a smidge late myself. My neighbor's little girl came down with a stomach bug. I had to run to the store to get her some Pedialyte and Rice Krispies, but I'm home now and will dress as fast as I can."

"No hurry. I'm a big boy. I can wait."

"I told Liz to go on ahead, she can make sure that Courtney doesn't come after you before I get there."

Liz? Oh, right. For just a moment, he'd forgotten that Emily's sister was in town early and joining them tonight. "I can handle Courtney in a crowd. It's alone that she worries me."

Emily's muffled laughter carried through the phone line. "I'll still get there as soon as I can."

"Thanks." With nothing else to add, they said their goodbyes and he slipped the phone into his breast pocket. Double-checking the room, he was definitely ready to get on with the show.

Some days, the idea of getting married just to get out of the bachelor auction didn't sound so bad. Most days, common sense ruled and he opted to keep Emily close to bail him out of trouble. So far that had worked just fine for him. No sense in fixing a system that wasn't broken. Keys in hand, he marched out of his condo and drove straight to the country club. Handing his car off to the valet, he sucked in a long breath and marched up the red-carpeted steps of the hundred-year-old edifice.

"Wait up." His cousin Porter trotted up the stairs. "Safety in numbers and all that."

"What are you worried about?" Devlin fell into step beside his cousin. "You're not the one on the auction block."

Clearing his throat, Porter shoved a finger in his collar and sighed. "I figure it's only a matter of time before Courtney of the many last names tires of bidding on you and Paige decides it's time for a different Baron to be on the auction block."

He should be so lucky.

"And when she does," Porter continued, "I'll be next in line."

"Say the word and I'll be happy to hand off the baton to you now. As a matter of fact, tonight would be a great test run."

"Not on your life." Porter flashed a cheeky grin. "If my luck holds, you'll stay a bachelor longer than George Clooney and Paige will find another way to raise big bucks for a worthy cause."

"Or pick on Colton."

"Or Cameron," Porter chuckled.

"There you go." Dev slapped his cousin on the shoulder and tipped his chin toward the bar. "I say we hide out at the bar until this shindig gets rolling."

"Works for me." Porter stuttered to a stop. "Oops. Grams is waving me over."

Their grandmother was standing beside two attractive women and no doubt was hoping that one of them would spark Porter's interest. Most likely the only reason she hadn't waved both of them over was because she knew Emily was his plus-one for the evening. Probably still believed, despite all their protests, that there was more to the relationship than friendship. Even though she was a woman, Emily had been one of his best friends for so many years, he couldn't imagine his life without her in it, but no matter the wishes of his family, neither he nor Emily felt any spark of romance. The memory of the one time they'd kissed and had both laughed so hard at the absurdity of a romantic relationship still brought a smile to his face. Some day, he hoped Emily found a man good enough for her. Then maybe his grandparents would finally understand that they really and truly were only good friends.

A chill passed over him, a cool breeze across the back of this neck. Glancing up, he searched for the air conditioning vents, considering if they were going to need to speak to maintenance about the room temperature. Not noticing any vents near him, he shook his head and scanned the room, his gaze landing on the double doorway into the grand ballroom. Blinking, he squeezed his eyes shut and focused once again on the doorway. His eyes had to be playing tricks on him. Had he ever seen Emily wear her hair like that? Swooped up on top of her head in a mop of curls that looked casual and yet determined, a few loose strands twirled around her neck. A long neck that curved ever so slightly at her bare shoulders.

Had she always had such a long kissable neck? And when had he ever thought of Emily's neck as kissable?

She took a few steps into the room, her gaze scanning the crowd. For a moment her eyes seemed to land on him, and his heart stuttered, making him feel like he needed to gasp for breath. Before he could wave her over, her gaze bounced to the other side of the dance floor. She straightened her shoulders, and even from this distance, he could see the hint of cleavage rise and fall as she breathed, and his heart shifted into high gear, pounding blood through his veins.

Dropping his gaze to the glass in his hand, he stared at the caramel colored liquid, sniffed at the contents and pressing his lips into a thin line, shook his head and lifted the glass toward the bartender. "What did you put in this?"

"Bourbon on the rocks. What you ordered."

Resisting the urge to take his own pulse, he nodded at the man and took a sip. Definitely bourbon. So why did Emily look so very different tonight?

Why is it that a new dress, a great hairdo, and a room filled with men in tuxedos always made the air sizzle with excitement? Liz could feel the energy to her core. This was definitely going to be a fun night. She'd promised her sister she would keep an eye on Devlin. The problem was that she'd only seen him in photos and suddenly, picking him out of the crowd wasn't as easy as she'd expected it to be.

For a second, she thought it might be him by the bar, but then she'd spotted another man on the dance floor who looked like the photos she'd seen. By the time she'd decided that was the wrong Baron, if he was a Baron at all, the first guy she'd pinpointed had turned his back to her. Only one way to find out. Careful not to trip over her own two feet, or her new shoes, she marched across the room toward the man nursing his drink at the counter.

The sandy-haired gentleman turned and their eyes locked. *Yep.* That was definitely the Devlin Baron that her sister had been hanging around with for more years than she could count. "Hi, handsome."

Devlin swallowed hard and proceeded to almost double over coughing.

"Sorry." Liz smacked his back. "Didn't mean to startle you."

"No," he shook his head vehemently, "just went down the wrong pipe."

Still patting his back more gently now, she nodded. "Better?"

Clearing his throat, he straightened and nodded his head.

"Lose your tie already?" She tried not to grin too widely.

"In my pocket." A moment later the tie dangled from his extended fingers.

"Let me." She moved in closer and would swear she watched him swallow his tongue. Again, she resisted the urge to chuckle. Considering how crappy her love life had been of late, it was nice to know she still could get some reaction from a man, even if it was choking to death. She turned and twisted the black silk fabric, and straightening the final product, tapped his chest and took a step back. "There you go."

"Thanks."

"Any time."

He stared and swallowed and Liz suspected if he was always this awkward, no wonder he needed Emily for a plus-one all the time. "Buy a girl a drink?"

"Sorry, yes, of course." He spun around and ordered a chocolate martini.

"Make that lemon drop instead, please." She smiled at the bartender and then shifted her attention to Devlin.

"I thought you hated lemon drop martinis? Too much like sucking on a lemon."

"That would be me." Emily sidled up beside Liz, and gave her a quick kiss on the cheek. "Thanks for covering."

By the time the two sisters had turned to face Devlin again, the man was staring slack jawed at both women, his gaze bouncing from his drink back to them before he spun on his heel and faced the bartender. "Are you sure there's only bourbon in this?"

Liz and her sister faced each other, mirror images of confusion visible when at the same moment they cracked up laughing.

For a quick second Devlin blinked then frowned. "What

the heck is going on here?"

Linking elbows with her sister, Emily grinned at her longtime friend. "I told you my sister was joining us tonight."

"Sister?"

Emily nodded. "You know that genetic thing when you share parents with another human being?"

"I know what 'sister' means." Shaking his head, Devlin sighed. "You're twins."

Liz and Emily bobbed their heads in unison.

"Identical twins."

Liz tipped her head toward her sister. "Your friend here is a smart guy."

Nodding, Emily returned her gaze to Devlin. "Sometimes."

"Wait a minute." Devlin held up his hand. "It is not my fault that you never mentioned your sister is a twin. Never mind an identical twin."

"I guess it never came up." Hefting a casual shrug, Emily smiled.

"Nice to meet you." Liz shot her arm straight out.

Devlin accepted her proffered hand and shook. "Pleasure is all mine."

"Okay, now that we've gotten introductions out of the way." Emily glanced over Dev's shoulder. "I could use a drink before the fun begins."

"Fun?" Liz waved a finger at the bartender.

"Chocolate martini, please," Emily ordered then shifted her weight to face her sister. "Every year, we have to fight off Courtney Miller from bidding on Devlin here."

"Why?" Liz glanced at Devlin and back. "What's wrong with Courtney Miller?"

"For one thing," Devlin took a short sip of his drink, "the woman is looking for husband number *four*."

"Ah." Now Liz understood. "And you want to be number one?"

"Right." Devlin frowned. "No. Wait."

Liz couldn't help but laugh out loud. He was cute when he was confused. Already this night was proving to be even more fun than she'd hoped for. And so was Devlin Baron.

CHAPTER THREE

ow had Emily's sister trapped him in his own words? It took a second but he finally laughed. "Let's just say I'm not interested in whatever Courtney has in mind."

"Got it." Liz nodded. "So what's the plan? Trip her when she walks by?"

If he thought it would work, Devlin just might have gone along with that one.

"You're thinking too hard on that, Devlin Baron." The reproving tone in Emily's voice was hard to miss.

"Isn't there someone else here we could hook her up with?" Devlin glanced around the room. Plenty of eligible men.

Liz followed his gaze. "You tell me. Who has more money than you?"

Devlin's head snapped around.

"Unless it's the sex she's after?" Liz smiled demurely at him. "Could that be it?"

"Don't mind my sister." Emily sighed. "She has no filter."

"I do too." Liz lifted her chin and straightened her shoulders which made her cleavage rise and fall again and Devlin resisted the urge to squirm. "I just happen to believe in telling it like it is."

"Like I said," Emily rolled her eyes skyward, "no filter."

"So how many men are rolling in money and sexy too, and which one would spark the husband-hunting woman's interest?" Liz pushed on.

Unfortunately, though there were plenty of rich and

handsome men in the room, many of them single, Courtney seemed almost obsessed with getting her hands on Devlin. Every year, he had to cough up more and more money to keep the woman's fake fingernails away from him.

"No one." Emily said what he'd been thinking. "At least no one that Courtney has shown any interest in."

"It's no use." Devlin understood all too well the thrill of the hunt. As far as he was concerned, for Courtney this was all about winning.

"Stuffed dates?" A waiter waved a tray of appetizers in front of them.

"Ooh." Liz waved her fingers over the tray until they snatched up a date. "I love stuffed dates."

The woman held it up to her lips and suddenly Devlin wished he were a date. The idea of Liz's mouth slowly devouring him was more thrilling than flying on the open seas in a sleek sailboat, or hitting the jackpot in the casino. Man, he needed to get his head on straight. Spinning around, he reached for his drink on the bar at the same time another waiter came by with a tray of caviar and sour cream. The collision sent the tray and the sour cream flying—onto Emily.

The surprised screech that escaped Emily's mouth sent a shiver up his spine as though someone had run their fingernails down a chalkboard. Her beautiful blue satin gown was dripping with black caviar and white sour cream.

Liz's "Oh, my," tumbled over the waiter's, "I'm so sorry, ma'am."

The flustered server mumbled something about a wet rag and took off across the room at a fast clip.

"I don't know what hurts more." Arms spread wide, Emily stared down at her food draped dress. "That I look like the inside of a blender or that a waiter old enough to be my father called me ma'am."

"You're going to need more than a rag. There have to be towels in the ladies' room. Let's boogie." Liz grabbed her sister by the arm and swooped her away.

At that very moment, the MC for the evening announced that this year the live bachelor auction would be starting off the evening's activities. Paige had mentioned something at dinner the other night that to avoid folks holding back on the silent auctions and other items, saving up to bid on the bachelors that they would auction the few men on the block first.

Devlin looked over his shoulder toward the hall where Emily and her sister had disappeared and prayed cleaning a dress wasn't going to take very long. A few feet away, he spotted Courtney Miller chatting with the auctioneer. The woman wore a sequined black gown that fit so snuggly he doubted she could sit. Maybe Liz's idea wasn't so bad. How hard would it be to trip a woman draped in black sequins?

"Good grief." Liz stared at her sister's food covered lap. "I'm not sure this is going to work."

"We have to try."

The loudspeakers in the bathroom softly announced the bachelor auction would be starting soon.

"And we have to make it fast." Emily grabbed several of the white terry washcloths neatly folded on the counter and began swiping at her dress.

"Careful!" Liz grabbed her arm. "Don't rub it in."

"I'm trying to rub it *off*."

"I get it." She grabbed fresh rags and began dabbing at the dress more carefully.

Again, the speakers announced for everyone to take their seats and the bachelors to report to the podium.

"Oh, boy." Emily glanced up at the speakers on the ceiling. "We're running out of time. What if we just pour water on it?"

"Why don't we just strip you down and wash it in the toilet?" Sometimes she wondered where her practical sister came up with such absurd ideas. "Just let me get rid of the bulk of this and we'll figure out what to do with the rest."

At that, the MC for the evening began reading the bios of the four bachelors up for auction.

"This is so not good." Emily shook her head and reached behind her back. "Get me out of this."

"What?" Liz waved her arms. "You planning on bidding for Devlin in your underwear?"

"No. I'm going to wash the dress."

"I don't think that's a good idea." Liz soaked one of the towels and began wiping at the sloppy skirt. "You could just go out there and bid in a dirty dress."

"Just what I need. To mingle with the cream of Houston's society looking like I've been dumpster diving." Sighing heavily, Emily twisted around. "Unzip me. We're going to rinse off the gunk and then dry it under the hand blower."

"It could make the stain worse."

"At least the whole skirt will be the same water-stained color." Emily twisted her arms over her shoulders. "Hurry."

As fast as she could, Liz shoved her sister into the nearest stall and helped her out of the flowing gown. "This would have been easier if you didn't dress like a Victorian lady-in-waiting."

"I do not," Emily huffed. "The sweetheart neckline is not Victorian."

"Maybe not, but it's still a discreet neckline. Add the long sleeves and no slit in the skirt, and I'd classify that if not Victorian, at least as conservative. My point being, if there were less dress it would be easier to clean and faster to dry."

The voice over the loudspeaker called Devlin Baron to the stage.

"Oh, hell." Emily flung the stall door open and ran across the empty ladies room. Taking hold of the dress now under the running faucet, she tipped her head at her sister. "Go to the table, grab my purse, and pull out the bidding number. You're going to have to bid for Dev. I'll finish up here and get out as fast as I can."

Liz nodded. What more could she do? "Do we have a limit?"

"Nope." Emily squeezed the water out of her dress and shook her head. "Whatever it takes to stop Courtney."

"Got it." Liz flung the door open and could hear the auctioneer opening the bidding at one thousand dollars. Scurrying across the room to their table, she listened as the bidding quickly jumped from one thousand to two and then twenty-five hundred and just as she yanked the number out of the purse, some woman with much too much make-up raised her hand to three thousand.

Liz made a dang good living, but who in their right mind would spend three grand for a dinner date with a man? Even if the man was Devlin Baron.

Standing at the table, her gaze shifting from the platform with Devlin standing at parade rest with his hands behind his back, and over to the bathroom door, hoping her sister would come out. She'd been given permission to bid as high as necessary, but at the moment three women, including the plastic face painted lady, had worked the bidding up to nine grand.

Who the heck pays that kind of money for a dinner date? She sucked in a breath, but no sign of her sister. Meanwhile, the bidding had reached twelve grand and at least one woman had the good sense to shake her head and back away from the bidding. Liz had watched enough episodes of that storage auction television show to know that if she jumped in too soon, all she would succeed at doing was raising the ante. Though, it didn't look like Devlin minded. His head turning slightly from side to side, his smile intact, silently wooing the audience, the guy didn't look like he had a care in the world.

One of the two women seemed to be slowing. The brunette had begun nibbling on her lower lip with every bid, and each rebuttal seemed to take a few seconds longer than the previous bid. Like it or not, there was no time for Emily, Liz was going to have to jump in. The plastic lady with a smug grin raised her card at twenty thousand dollars and the brunette's shoulders slumped and her card face down at her table, she shook her head. She was out.

Even though the idea of twenty thousand dollars gave her goose flesh, it was her turn. The auctioneer called for twenty-one thousand and sucking in a long deep breath while she prayed she didn't pass out, even if she was spending someone else's money, she raised her card.

The auctioneer acknowledged the bid and the blonde's head snapped around so fast that Liz thought it might fall off her shoulders.

Liz couldn't help but chuckle to herself. Wouldn't that be a cheap resolution for Devlin if the barracuda lady simply lost her head?

CHAPTER FOUR

Where the heck was Emily? It was taking every ounce of his poker face skills to keep from showing just how nervous he actually was. Two of the three serious bidders had fallen by the wayside and any second now, he was going to be at the mercy of Courtney Miller.

"Do I hear twenty-one?" At least that's what Dev thought the auctioneer had said. The man had been told not to go as fast as a traditional bidding scenario, but a few times he'd rambled on so quickly, Devlin had lost track of where the bidding was.

To Dev's relief, a card went up. Only it wasn't Emily. Her sister was calling the shots. Not that he cared. As long as he didn't have to deal with Courtney, he didn't care which of the Carter twins bid on him.

More challenging than not letting the crowd see him sweat was not bursting out with laughter at the look on Courtney's face when Liz waved her number with every increase. Courtney's shock had transitioned to irritation, and now that the bidding was up to thirty thousand, he expected smoke to blow out of her ears any second now.

How he wished Emily were here to see the show. Last year, Courtney had walked away when the bidding reached thirty. She must be seriously ticked off to be pushing thirty-five now. For just a flash, he wondered if this was the year that she would stay in the game until Emily, or Liz, backed down. A few more waves and the two women seemed to have lost track of the money and were staring each other down clearly determined to win. Once again, Dev's nerves were beginning to snap at him. All he could do is pray that

Liz didn't chicken out.

"Going, going…" the auctioneer's voice penetrated the thoughts scrambling around in Devlin's head. "And sold for thirty-seven thousand dollars."

The room erupted in catcalls and applause, and Devlin's gaze snapped around to Emily coming into the room, looking around and, her gaze meeting Devlin, she shrugged. That could not be good. Liz was gone from the table, and quickly scanning the rest of the room he spotted Courtney marching out the door.

What he couldn't determine is who had lost and who was going to pay the bill, and considering Emily had his checkbook, his gut clenched at the thought that Courtney might be paying for him right this minute.

Nodding politely at all the guests still applauding and the MC carrying on over what a wonderful success tonight would be now that Devlin got the ball rolling, he strolled as casually as he could over to Emily. Even if what he really wanted was to sprint across the grand hall and if it turned out Courtney had won the bid, join his cousin Kyle on the family racing yacht and not stop till they reached somewhere safe, like Timbuktu.

The moment he reached his longtime friend, he glanced down at her dress. The sour cream was gone, but he could see streaks of light and dark where the gown was still wet. "You all right?"

"I've been better."

At the same moment, their voices tumbled over each other, "What happened?"

"You don't know?" Emily's brows curved over the bridge of her nose. "You were there."

"I was distracted. Didn't you see?"

She shook her head. "No. I couldn't tell who was winning the bets from inside the ladies room and by the time I made it back here it was all over. Where's Liz?"

"I saw her leaving through one door and Courtney through another. Does she have my checkbook?"

"It was in my purse. I don't know if she grabbed it with my bidding number or not."

"Well, there's only one way to find out." Though he didn't understand why both women had disappeared and why one of them wasn't here either congratulating him for sliding by or gloating for finally winning.

"Let me grab my purse." Emily didn't wait for him, and even though he didn't want to delay the inevitable, he followed her to the table. Quickly, she snapped her purse open and glanced inside. "Your checkbook is still here."

"Dang it." That was so not a good sign. It would have been worth every penny to him not to have to deal with Courtney the Barracuda.

Liz appeared at her sister's side. "Why do you two look so glum?"

Her sister held up Devlin's checkbook before handing it over to him. "Because you lost."

"Lost?" Frowning, Liz glanced from her sister to Devlin.

Taking a step back, Emily turned to Devlin. "Excuse me, but now that you don't need me any more, I'm going home and getting out of this wet—and dirty—dress. Besides," she waved a thumb at her sister, "I hate the sight of blood."

Staring at her sister's departing back, before either of them could say another word, Courtney sidled up to Liz. "Next time, he's mine." Spinning around, she leaned into Devlin, ran her very long and shiny red fingernail along his chin, and licked her lips. "Darling, if you're ever in need of a real woman, you know where to find me."

Watching her strut away, Devlin waited till she was engrossed in conversation with a group of cackling women before turning to Liz and flashing his very best smile. "Sorry I ever doubted you two."

"Two?" Liz slapped her hand across her nicely exposed cleavage. "I'll have you know I learned how to count in kindergarten and haven't forgotten. I didn't need big sister to accomplish this mission."

"Forgive me. And thank you." Dev opened his checkbook and scribbled her name and the winning amount, or what he thought was the winning amount with a small bonus for the trouble, and ripped the check out. "Here you go. And again, thank you."

Liz shook her head and held her hand up. "Oh no you don't. I won you. Fair. And. Square."

The only thing more fun than getting caught up in the bidding war with the plastic blonde was the look on Devlin's face right now. If it were humanly possible, his jaw would have scraped the ground.

"Elizabeth Louise," her sister plopped her hands on her hips and snapped her jaw shut. "Have you lost your mind?"

Probably. She'd just about maxed out her credit card, and no doubt it would take her forever to pay off the debt, but suddenly the idea of dining out with a man who could afford to spend that kind of money at the drop of a hat sounded like too much fun to resist.

"How about a compromise?" Devlin still held the check in his hand.

"Such as?"

"We go on the date with a billionaire as advertised…"

She waited for the rest of what he had to say.

"And you let me reimburse you for saving me from the Barracuda."

That was seriously tempting. Especially since never in her life had she run her credit card bills that high. At least not her personal card. She'd spent small fortunes for work but that was always reimbursed by the clients, usually with a slight profit.

"What do you say?"

"Let me think about it." She grinned at him.

"Liz!" Emily, always practical and rarely willing to take a risk, frowned at her twin.

A low rumble of a laugh escaped her lips. "All right. I'll accept the check. But we agree that I still get the whole shebang?"

Still holding the check with one hand, he crossed his

heart with the other. "Yes, ma'am, or hope to die."

"Don't do that." Liz chuckled more loudly and folding the check, slipped it into her cleavage. Glancing up, she noticed Devlin's eyes had rounded wider than an owl with insomnia. "Don't worry, I'll put it in my purse when I get back to the table."

"Oh, I…" Devlin looked to Emily who merely rolled her eyes and Devlin sighed. "Sorry."

"Come on." Liz laughed and stretched her hand out. "Let's grab a snack while these crazy people bid on the rest of the bachelors."

"Crazy?" Again, Devlin glanced at her sister.

"What else would you call someone willing to drop five figures on a dinner date?"

This time Devlin laughed loudly. "When you put it that way…"

"Coming with us, sis?" Liz smiled at Emily.

"I think I've had enough excitement for one night." She turned to face Devlin. "If you're willing to see her home, I think I'm going to call it an early night and get out of this damp dress."

"Of course." Devlin nodded.

"All right." Liz looked over to the spread of food in the adjoining salon and slapping her hands together, smiled. "Suddenly, I'm starved."

And Devlin had never been more confused in his life. Where Emily was a calm and comforting force in his life, her sister Liz was a bloody tornado. The two might look similar at first glance, but the two women couldn't be more different, and only one made his heart race faster than a thoroughbred at the derby.

"Ooh, look." Liz had a plate in hand and was perusing the choices. "I love little meatballs." She stabbed one with a toothpick and shoved it in her mouth. "Oh, they're better than they look. Try one." She stabbed at another, spun around and waved it in Devlin's face.

All he could do was bite it off the toothpick before anyone noticed the interaction.

The auctioneer's voice reached where they stood. "Sold for fifteen thousand."

Liz stopped and holding an empty plate in one hand and a toothpick in the other, glanced over to where Devlin had been standing two bids ago. "Wow. You really do command top dollar."

"If you take Courtney out of the mix, I'd probably not earn so much money for the charity."

Plopping two or three more hors d'oeuvres onto her plate, she paused and tipped her head to one side, studying Devlin. "Wouldn't it be easier to simply make a donation and skip the performance?"

He'd asked himself that same thing more than once over the last few years. "I have, but my family has a soft spot for all charities related to foster kids, so someone has to participate."

"I suppose." She frowned and jabbed at a stuffed mushroom.

The woman had a healthy appetite. Dinner may prove to be more costly than he'd anticipated. "The other thing is that letting Courtney bid helps set the mood."

"Mood? For murder?" She chuckled softly before shoving the mushroom into her mouth in a single bite.

"No." Though some days he did wonder. "Her crazy high bidding sets an example for the folks with disposable income to cough up more of it than they'd intended. And that's good for the charity."

"It is." She nodded her agreement. "You know what this needs?" She waved her hand at the food on her plate.

"Ketchup?"

She rolled her eyes. "Bite your tongue. I was thinking a glass of wine."

"There's plenty of free booze around here."

"Wouldn't the charity make more if they charged for it?"

He shrugged. "Maybe, but tipsy people are more free

with their checkbooks."

"Ah." She waved that toothpick around, this time with a stuffed date on the end. "Makes good sense."

"Glad you approve."

Her smile broadened and she cast a sideways glance in his direction. "You're not what I expected."

"How so?"

She shrugged. "Not sure yet, but I'll let you know when I figure it out."

Liz wasn't the only one with something to figure out. Understanding women was not something that came naturally to most men and Dev was no exception. But right now, he was more than willing to give it a try. If he survived.

CHAPTER FIVE

"**D**id you win the lottery and forget to tell me?" Hands on her hips, elbows sticking out like chicken wings, Emily scanned the bags and clothes scattered across the bed.

"For years, you've talked about Devlin this, Devlin that. For as much as I've heard, I actually know very little." Setting down the black sheath dress she'd picked out, among many, she held up one hand and began picking off fingers with the other. "Handsome as sin—which we know at least the barracuda agrees with you. Successful—anyone willing to drop five digits on dinner had better be successful or else he's certifiable. Loves his family—that one I'll take your word for, but I think it says a lot about the man. He's a sharp dresser—hence hitting every sales rack at Nordstrom's and Neiman's." She waved the same hand that had been counting fingers, across the width of the bed.

"Don't go setting your sights on Devlin Baron, the man is as much a perpetual bachelor as Warren Beatty or Leonardo DiCaprio. Except, of course, Devlin doesn't date teenyboppers."

"And Warren Beatty is married now."

"That's not the point. He didn't marry young so, enjoy your dinner and call it a day."

"Have you changed your mind about him?" At first Liz had thought that her twin had a crush on her handsome plus-one. Eventually, Liz figured out they were truly good friends, but maybe she'd been wrong.

"About what?" Emily's gaze remained fixed on all the merchandise scattered across the bed.

"Not what. Who. Devlin."

Emily's head snapped around. "For the love of Jehoshaphat. Now I know you've lost your mind."

It took Liz a long few moments to determine the expression on her sister's face. In the end, love wasn't it. The woman was truly exasperated with her twin. "Fine. So what's the problem?"

"The problem is." Emily picked up the strappy stiletto shoes with sparkles across one strap. "I love you both and don't want to see anyone getting hurt."

"Hurt? Why would we get hurt?"

"For one thing, you wouldn't be the first woman swept away by the Baron lifestyle."

"Lifestyle? It's a dinner date. A bought and paid for dinner date, not even a hint of invitation there."

"You say that now, but I've seen women fall over him when they realize how much money the Barons have. Then there's Devlin."

"What about him?"

"He's a nice guy. Nicer than most people realize, and he takes family very seriously. Love too, which is probably why he isn't married. I've seen the crushed look in his eyes when he really likes someone, I mean really, and then he realizes the only thing they love back about him is his bank account."

"And you think I'm after his money?" Liz didn't know whether to take her sister's temperature or smack her upside the head.

"I know you're not after his money, but I also know that you're smart, and pretty, and flaunt it in a way that I never could. Even back in high school, boys would fall all over themselves to get your attention and not notice I was standing right there too. You have that way about you and I don't want Devlin getting caught up in it."

The serious tone of Emily's voice and deep concern in her eyes reminded Liz so much of how even as little kids, Emily always protected her. "Don't worry. This is just a fun chance to live like the other half I've been watching for years. Come Monday morning, I'm back to working nine to five and only getting glimpses into the wealthy's homes, lifestyles, and budgets."

Emily studied her sister.

"I promise. All will be well."

Sighing, Emily turned her head back to the bed. "Then wear this one." She held up the black dress. "Black goes with everything and it will show off your legs."

"Done." Liz threw here arms around her sister. "I love you."

"Love you more," Emily whispered, then pulled back. "Now get dressed. I forgot to mention that Devlin is always punctual."

Never in her life had Liz gotten ready for a date, or sort-of date, so fast. There was no way she wanted to keep Devlin waiting and she'd spent more time than she'd meant to at the mall this afternoon. Taking a last-minute look in the mirrored closet doors, she had to admit, the black dress was the right choice. She could fit in anywhere that Devlin took them.

The doorbell sounded and Liz swallowed hard. This wasn't exactly a real date, so why the heck was her stomach fluttering more than when the captain of the football team asked her to the homecoming dance?

In all the years that Devlin had picked Emily up for one event or other, never had he ever felt like swallowing his tongue. How could the two sisters be identical twins and yet look so very different. Not just the fashion, but the way they carried themselves. He'd always found Emily to be an attractive, well-dressed woman whom he was proud to have on his arm, but Liz? Liz made him feel like he'd fallen into a vat of peanut butter. His limbs too heavy to lift and his tongue stuck to the roof of his mouth.

"You're right on time." Even Liz's smile was the same yet different. There was a twinkle in her eyes, almost mischievous, that made it hard to look away.

"Do my best." For a fraction of a moment, he debated

what to do next. This wasn't really a date and yet it was. When in doubt, remember everything his grandmother and grandfather and parents ever taught him about being a gentleman. Which meant extending his elbow to her. "Shall we?"

The way Liz glanced down at his arm, for a few seconds, she seemed to be weighing whether or not it would bite her. In another beat, her gaze lifted to his, her smile broadened, and her hand curled around his elbow. "All set."

There had barely been enough time to close the passenger door behind Liz when Devlin's phone dinged. Scurrying around the hood of the car, he pulled his phone out of his pocket. In the front seat, he snapped his seat belt in place with one hand and scanned the text with his other. "Blast."

A frown creased Liz's brow.

"I hate to say this, but we have to make a quick stop."

Lips pressed tightly together, her head bobbed. She was doing the same thing Emily did, studying him, measuring her words.

"It's the alarm company on a new project."

Her one brow shot up.

"There may have been a break in. The alarm sounded and the police are on their way."

"Is it far?"

"No." He shook his head. "About five minutes." If he pushed the car and the lights cooperated.

Her gaze on the road, Liz didn't say a word, which suited him just fine at the moment. His mind was reeling with possibilities of what he would, or would not, find. The city traffic lights were on his side tonight. Every one was green or yellow as he approached and they made it to the house in just a few minutes. Multiple police cars were already parked in front and his stomach did a momentary dive.

"Shall I wait here?"

He considered for a moment if she'd be safer here alone or inside with him. Since all the police seemed to be in the house, inside made more sense. "Lousy way to start a dinner date, but we might as well face whatever awaits together."

"Safety in numbers," she teased softly.

Despite the bird swooping in his stomach at the thought of the potential damage that might greet him, her words were exactly what he needed to relax a smidgeon and even drew a small smile from him.

The front door wide open, he sucked in a deep breath and without thinking, reached for Liz's hand as if it had been his longtime friend with him and not her sister.

"Oh," Liz spoke first. "This is lovely."

His gaze quickly danced across the entry and view of the living room to spot an officer with a flashlight in hand coming toward them.

"Mr. Baron?"

Devlin nodded.

"We've checked the premises, upstairs and down. Whoever broke in isn't here now. Can you tell if anything is missing?"

Another officer came from the kitchen, and Devlin could see a couple more officers in the backyard. "My assistant would know better than I would. Is there any damage?"

The officer shook his head. "If you're asking me if your a/c unit is gone or holes in your walls, no."

That was a relief.

"May I look around?"

Turning to face the officer, before Devlin could say anything, the policeman nodded at him. When he spun around to talk to Liz, he realized she was actually waiting for him to let go of her hand. Gently letting go and taking a step in retreat, he sighed. "Sorry, please feel free to walk around. I'll catch up with you in a minute."

It took all of five more minutes to get an update from the police and him to find Liz upstairs.

"Nice house. Anything missing?"

"I don't think so, but my assistant will have a list of staged items."

Bobbing her head, she took in the spacious game room. "I thought you did commercial development?"

"Normally, yes. Not too long ago a friend of mine approached me with an opportunity to buy out a builder who had gone belly up. He'd built one spec house and was putting up two more when, thanks to a messy divorce, his finances went south and he had to shut down. Once the divorce was settled, the three houses and several lots became available for a song."

"And you can't resist a good deal." She smiled.

"Emily mention that?" He grinned back, liking the way she seemed to like what she was seeing.

Her smile widened. "Among other things."

"Uh-oh." He crossed his arms. "Would you like a guided tour of the rest of the house?"

"I'd love it, but," she paused at a built-in bookshelf, "mind if I move something first?"

"Move?"

Shaking her head, she backed away from the shelving. "Never mind."

"No. I wasn't following you."

"Have you ever heard the expression 'less is more'?"

He nodded.

"It applies to staging. Sometimes if a stager over fills the house with tchotchkes, it can distract home buyers, and not always in a good way."

"I see." Not that he had any idea why knick-knacks mattered.

"Watch." She raised her hand at him before walking away. "Close your eyes."

He did as he was told.

"Okay. Open them."

Blinking a couple of times, he studied the shelf, then he looked at the matching one on the other side. She was right. There was too much on the other shelving. One unit had just enough to highlight it—the other one had him looking at all the decorations and not at the house. "How do you know this?"

She chuckled. "Has my big sister not mentioned that I'm an interior decorator?"

"No." At least he didn't think so. Stifling a laugh, he shrugged at her. "Maybe?"

CHAPTER SIX

What started out as moving a few pieces out of the way swiftly became a redesign session. Together, they started removing the extra knick-knacks and soon wound up rearranging furniture and placing the pieces she thought were superfluous into the garage. "You should be able to call the staging company and have them pick up the unwanted items from the garage. No point in paying for what you don't need."

"It's funny how moving the chairs away from the fireplace make this room so much more inviting."

It delighted her to no end that he appreciated what she'd done. "So glad you like the changes."

"Very much." He nodded. "You should open a staging business. Houston is woefully behind other cities with staging options."

"That's actually why I'm here."

He cocked his head to one side. "To start a new business?"

"No." She chuckled softly. "I have a client who decided to venture out into flipping houses in Houston. Until he decides if he's going to do more houses here or not, he's bringing his team in. In only a few days, I've managed to figure out it's not going to be as easy as I like. We may wind up just buying the pieces I want and offering them for sale later."

"That might have been cheaper than what I'm paying for this house."

"Back home, we have top-notch choices in quality furniture and accessories. Here, I'm not finding the type of pieces I need to showcase without overwhelming."

"I can see it's not as easy as it looks."

At the exact moment she shook her head, her stomach rumbled.

Devlin glanced at his wrist. "Wow. I didn't realize how long we'd been putzing around. We'd better get moving."

Slinging her purse over her shoulder, she followed him to the front door. "Are we too late for our reservation?"

"Reservations are only a formality. Even if we're a little late, Stuart will find us a table."

"Is he a friend of yours?" She passed him, stepping out onto the porch.

"I've known him since college." Devlin turned to lock the door and place the keys in the realtor box. "He owns one of the best steak houses in Houston. Some of my best business deals were negotiated over a rib eye and burned corn."

"I'm sorry. Burned corn? Can't be that good of a restaurant."

A soft chuckle filled the air. "Don't let the name fool you. It's absolutely delicious. The whole family agrees, they've been dining there for years so Stuart is pretty much a friend of every member of the family."

"Oh, good. I've worked up a bit of an appetite." A bit might have been somewhat of an understatement. Right about now, she was hungry enough to eat a side of beef all by herself.

Settled into the car, Devlin latched his seat belt and pushed the ignition button. "We'll be there in about fifteen minutes."

"Oh?" She secured her own seat belt. "It's close."

A grin spread across Devlin's face as a twinkle shone in his eyes. "Let's say I know a few shortcuts."

What the man probably knew was how to win the Indy 500. She didn't notice how fast he was driving until he took the last corner on two wheels. Or at least what felt like two wheels. She should have realized any man who picks a woman up in a low to the ground sports car was going to push the engine to the limits. Though it was kind of sweet that he was in a hurry because she was hungry.

"We're almost there." Devlin eased the car to a stop at a traffic light. The whirl of a siren sounded and he glanced into the rear-view mirror. Colored lights reflected off the dashboard and Dev inched the car closer to the curb.

For a split second she wondered if he had been driving even faster than she'd thought, but she quickly realized the source of the siren had nothing to do with Devlin's driving and everything to do with the fire department. Despite the power that she was sure came with the Baron name, it was kind of nice to see that he was not only respectful of the law, but at least to some extent, a rule follower.

One fire engine flew past them and then another smaller truck followed by a police car. "That can't be good for someone."

Devlin shook his head. For a second he closed his eyes and she realized he was saying a silent prayer. Why she wouldn't have expected that from such a prominent wealthy man, she didn't know, but closing her own eyes and thanking God for protecting whoever was in trouble, she took another second to thank him for letting her meet Devlin Baron. She had a feeling getting to know this most eligible bachelor was going to be enlightening.

The light flashed to green and Devlin stepped on the gas pedal a little less forcefully than before. The problem as she saw it though, was that the closer they got to their destination, the more emergency vehicles flew by, slowing their progress. Another few blocks and the problem became very clear. Black smoke filled the night air. "Someone's not having a good night."

Dev shook his head. "That's a lot of smoke and a lot of fire trucks. Whatever it is, it's big."

She couldn't argue with that. The burning stench filled the car.

Another couple of blocks and the muscles along Devlin's jawline began to twitch. "Damn it."

"What's wrong?" Her gaze scanned the horizon, more specifically, the cluster of emergency vehicles stopped ahead.

"The Steer's Den is on fire."

"Steer's Den?" she muttered softly, but she was pretty sure she already knew what that meant.

"Stuart's restaurant *is* the Steer's Den."

Flames shot up into the air higher than Liz had ever seen. Black smoke filled the night air. With more and more emergency vehicles arriving, Devlin couldn't bring his car anywhere near as close to the restaurant.

"Now what?" Liz gawked at the flames dancing along the rooftops up the street. "It seems to be spreading."

"I need to make sure everyone is all right." Glancing over his shoulder, he looked left then right and pulled the car over to the curb.

The concern in his eyes would have been obvious to any idiot. Though she had no idea what he could do that the firemen and EMTs weren't already doing, she nodded and unfastened her seat belt.

"No. You stay here."

"If there's anything I can do, I want to do it."

Already standing outside the car, he tapped the roof and nodded. "Thanks. I'll be back in a minute."

From where she stood, she saw him cross the barricade the emergency vehicles had set up, and a fireman with a walkie-talkie at his mouth stop him. There seemed to be some vehement words as arms moved and pointed and chins jutted forward. Reaching into his breast pocket, Devlin waved his wallet in the man's face. Suddenly, the wide ranged arm motions stopped and the fireman turned his back to Devlin, pointing in a different direction.

Apparently, there were more perks to being a Baron than she'd figured on. What else was there about the Barons, especially Devlin Baron, that she didn't know about?

Not that he could replace the firemen or the EMTs, but Devlin was a Baron, and sometimes, that made things happen faster or more effectively than they might under ordinary circumstances. Promising the captain he would stay out of the way, the man finally gave in and told Devlin that everyone had been evacuated safely, and pointed to where they were being triaged on the other side of the fire trucks.

Looking back to where he'd left the car, he could see Liz on her feet, straining to see what was going on. Bless her, she'd stayed back as he'd asked her to, but he couldn't leave her there and check on what he wanted to. Trotting back to the car, he grabbed for her hand. "Come on. It looks like everyone's out, but I still want to see for myself they're all right."

Slamming the door behind her, she hurried after him, matching her gait to his longer one. Deep down he knew he should slow down, but he needed to make sure Stuart and all his staff were safe and had all they needed.

Hurrying around the cluster of firetrucks, he ducked behind the first EMT truck. A woman sat on a stretcher, inhaling oxygen, with one EMT monitoring her while his partner checked another woman sitting on the floor. The lady on the floor seemed to be in better shape than the woman with the oxygen mask. "Have you seen Stuart?"

"He was the last one out." The girl, probably in her early twenties and a newer server since Dev didn't recognize her, pointed over her shoulder. "He's being difficult."

That's just one of the things Devlin was afraid of. Forcing himself to walk at a reasonable pace, he didn't let go of Liz's hand. He had no idea if she cared or not, but right now he had a singular focus and didn't want to add worrying about Liz to the list.

"Is that him?" Liz waved her free arm near another EMT truck.

Lifting his gaze in the same direction Liz pointed, he spotted a tall male figure shouting and waving his arms, clearly giving the EMT a hard time. "Yep. That's Stuart."

He'd taken one step, maybe two, when he heard shouting and spotted the firemen hurrying away from the building as a loud crunching sound echoed around them.

Looking up at the old restaurant, the flames shot up higher than he'd ever seen. A boom followed the crunch and bursting flames, and in the blink of an eye the roof collapsed.

There was no mistaking the echoing sound of a male voice, probably the captain, shouting for his men to report in. One by one he heard the muffled voices of men identifying themselves. Another moment and there was more frantic yelling, a hose shifting to pour water at a different spot, and another few breathless moments and two firemen came out the doorway under a rush of water, one leaning heavily on the other.

Dev could almost feel the sigh of relief embrace him as more firemen ran and the one man, pulling away from his partner, limped over to the waiting EMT.

"Oh, thank god." Shaking her head, Liz pressed her lips tightly together before facing him again. "It's a miracle no one got hurt."

"I was just thinking the same thing."

"I'm fine, damn it." Stuart's voice climbing over the hum of noise around them snapped Devlin's thoughts away from the building collapse and back to the scramble of restaurant staff.

"Stuart," Devlin called out as he and Liz trotted over to him. "What do you think you're doing?"

"I need to get to the hospital."

"That's what we've been telling him," the EMT fighting with him shouted over the noise around them.

"Not me." Stuart practically growled at the man. "They've taken half my people to the hospital."

"Just as a precaution. There are no serious injuries, except for your arm. Now will you *please* let me take a look?" The EMT reached for Stuart's right arm.

The fabric was torn and it was clear his arm was badly burned. That had Dev's gaze drifting to Stuart's other arm. The shirt also torn, his hand had less severe burns. "What the heck happened?"

"I had to get everyone out. Sarah was petrified. Literally. She stared at the flames in the storage room and wouldn't move. I had to douse us in water and practically carry her out."

"And then he ran back in to make sure no one was left behind." One of the regular waiters that Dev recognized came to stand beside them.

"How ya feeling, Tom?" Concerned with his employee, Stuart forgot about the EMT and let the guy check his arm and his vitals.

"I'm fine. Not a scratch on me. I did a head count," Tom said. "Everyone is accounted for and you're the only one injured."

"What about Mary? She's on oxygen." Stuart's gaze skipped to the other EMT vehicle where they'd seen the woman on a stretcher on oxygen.

"Just a precaution," the EMT responded, wrapping a blood pressure cuff on Stuart's arm.

"She has asthma." Stuart closed his eyes.

"We know. Like I said, a precaution."

With that, the doors closed on the vehicle holding Mary and pulled away.

"What can I do?" Dev asked.

Stuart shook his head. "I have no idea right now."

"Are you insured?"

This time his friend nodded. "It happened so fast. It was insane. The smoke was so thick."

"I know." Dev patted the man's good shoulder.

"Your BP is through the roof." The EMT folded up the blood pressure cuff.

"No, surprise there." Stuart rolled his eyes.

"We need to get you to the hospital, treat that arm, monitor your BP, and…" the EMT raised his hand before Stuart could protest, "this way you can check on your people yourself."

Stuart nodded. "Okay. Good idea."

"I'll call you in the morning. See how you're doing," Devlin said.

"Thanks." Stuart tried to smile but only one corner of his mouth barely moved. "Sorry about your reservation."

Dev couldn't help but chuckle, and thankfully, that

pulled a slight smile from Stuart. "It'll be all right."

Stuart sighed. "Let's hope the insurance company agrees."

"We'll talk in the morning." Dev took a step back. "Go take care of yourself." He stood still until the vehicle pulled away with Stuart inside. Spinning around, he realized he was still holding Liz's hand. What a way to start an evening out. He was going to have to make this up to her. "Hungry?"

CHAPTER SEVEN

The short walk back to their car went more slowly than the rushed steps when they'd first arrived. Liz could tell Devlin was processing the evening. The way the muscles in his jaw clenched, she knew the situation and concern for his friend had him more than a little unsettled.

At his car, the same way as he'd done when he'd first picked her up and then again after the spec house, he opened her door and offering a hand, waited for her to climb in before closing the door and circling the hood to the driver side.

Nothing about tonight was happening the way she'd expected, and right about now, she wished she could do something for Devlin besides rearrange the staging in his residential project.

In his seat, Devlin pushed the button to start the car and blew out a deep sigh. "Still up for steak?"

She really wished he didn't seem so worn out. "You don't really want to eat. You're still worried about Stuart."

Devlin's head snapped around. "It shows?"

"I've got great instincts." Sucking in a deep breath of her own, she reached over and touched the top of his hand. It had been nice having his hand wrapped with hers for the last hour or so. "Why don't we head to the hospital and I can get a lift from there back to my sister's."

"No, ma'am. My grandmother would have my hide if I let you take a public ride home."

"Okay, what if you drop me off at the condo and then you go to the hospital and check on your friend."

He shook his head. "I promised you a dinner date."

"We can do dinner another night."

"You're probably starved." Devlin pulled away from the curb. "Tomorrow morning will be soon enough to deal with the aftermath of the fire. I'm sure Stuart will be fine once the adrenaline rush dies down."

"You keep telling yourself that." She leaned back in her seat. This man was proving to be very interesting in ways she'd never imagined. "Let's try something different."

"I'm all ears." He kept his gaze on the road ahead.

"We'll go to the hospital. You can do whatever you need to. Then I have an idea for where to go for dinner."

His gaze shifted to level with hers. "You don't mind?"

"Not at all. Friends are important and you'll feel better once you see for yourself that all is in order."

"I guess you're about to get a tour of the ER at County Medical."

The smile on his face made giving up a fancy night out worth it. Watching Devlin stroll into the hospital like he owned the place was not what she'd expected once they arrived. Though, now that she thought about it, she knew his family name was a big deal, she should have known he, and all the other Barons probably did own half the city.

"I'm looking for Stuart Whitman."

The woman at the desk began clacking on the keyboard. "Are you family?"

Devlin shook his head.

"I'm sorry sir. I'm only allowed to give information to immediate family."

This time, Devlin nodded and turned away.

For a split second Liz thought that was all there was to it. They would leave and get something to eat and Devlin would call Stuart or whoever in the morning. Only Devlin didn't walk to the door, he stopped in the hall and pulled out his phone. Whether he was talking to the real governor or his grandfather, she didn't know. What she did know was that when Devlin finished with two more short phone calls, a distinguished man in a suit with graying temples came up to them. A handshake and a few quick words, and the hospital director escorted them into the ER.

Liz was getting an up close and personal tour, not of the hospital, but of the influence the Baron name held. Try as she might, she wasn't quite sure what to make of it all. Though she was pretty sure about at least one thing. This man wasn't going through the motions of doing the right thing, he clearly really cared about people. All of his questions were not just about the treatment everyone was getting, he was concerned if they all had enough health insurance, he put in a few calls to people about speeding up the insurance claim for the building, and by the time they'd made it back to the car, he'd already made arrangements for a temporary location for the restaurant to open in so that none of the employees would be out of work.

Damn that man was good. Too good to be true.

"Now I'm starving." Sliding into the car, Devlin leaned back against the headrest for just a second.

"A good day's work will do that to you. Is your life always this… intense?"

"Intense?"

"Having your new spec house broken into was quite a bit of excitement for one night, but no, you had a break in and a fire. It's enough to make a person's head spin. Or buy a rabbit's foot."

He chuckled at the lucky rabbit's foot, though she had a point, he might just have to buy one. His mind still racing at a thousand miles an hour, he shook his head. There was still so much to work out in order for Steer's Den to move forward, for him the next twenty-four hours didn't hold out hope of being any easier. "Thank God, no. I feel like today has had seventy-two hours in it. And to make matters worse, most restaurants are closed now."

"Not all. I think I have the perfect solution for your latest dilemma." Liz shifted in her seat, her gaze straight ahead.

"Where to?" No doubt, Liz had to be starving now too.

"You'll see when we get there." A hint of a smile tugging at the corners of her mouth, she clasped her hands together and continued to keep her eyes forward.

"A secretive streak?" This woman was full of surprises.

She shrugged at him and her smile widened. "Take Westminster to Marietta."

"Yes, ma'am." Normally, he would be taken aback by the secretiveness. Being taken blind into a situation was not in his comfort zone, but right now he was more intrigued than irritated. Maybe it was because he was exhausted, or maybe it was the company. Either way, he was looking forward to finding out where she was taking him to eat. Actually, he was downright intrigued by the prospect of being led into the unknown. How ridiculous was that.

On Marietta Avenue and a few more turns had them deep in the heart of one of the oldest Houston neighborhoods. Between work and time with family at the ranch, it had been years since he'd been down this way.

"There." Liz pointed to the corner. "Pull into that parking lot."

The neon sign for Kelly's Burgers flashed at him. "They're still open?"

"Till two am."

"How'd you know about this place?"

"Emily brought me here on my last visit. Best burger I'd ever had."

"You really want to eat at a greasy spoon?"

"If the burgers and fries are as good as last time I was here, yes."

In the parking lot attached to one of the oldest family owned burger joints in the county, he removed his jacket and tie and set them in the back seat, then rolled up his sleeves. "Let's go."

This time he resisted the urge to grab hold of her hand. Inside they settled into a booth near the far corner. He doubted the place had changed in the last fifty or so years.

"Did you know that this place has been in the Kelly family since it opened?" Liz didn't look up from the menu.

"I went to school with Cynthia Kelly. Her grandfather

started this place. We used to go to the Kelly's in north Houston. Though it's not as nostalgic as this place."

"I love the décor. It reminds me of an old diner."

A waitress with her hair in a netted bun paused at the table, setting two glasses of ice water in front of them. "Would you like anything else to drink?"

Liz grinned up at the woman. "I'll have a cola, no ice, a mushroom cheeseburger, no onions, and the sweet potato chips, please."

"What kind of cheese?" the woman scribbled on a pad and didn't glance up.

"Swiss."

"Got it. And you, sir?" This time the woman looked at him and for just a second, he thought she seemed familiar.

"The same. Except I'll have ice in my drink, please." For an instant, he thought he saw recognition in the woman's eyes as well. Now that was going to nag at him.

"Are you all right?" Liz stretched her hand out and gently covered his for too short a moment.

"Yes, sorry. I was distracted."

"Still worrying about Stuart?"

"Actually, no. I think we've got that all worked out. Though it was a relief to discover his burns weren't severe enough to keep him in the hospital, so tomorrow we'll meet at the commercial location and see how fast we can get him back in business."

"It was fascinating watching you work." Pushing back in her seat, Liz pulled her hand away, something he instantly regretted.

Stretching for the water glass to give the hand missing her touch something to do besides reach for her, he chuckled softly. "You never watched anyone talk on the phone—a lot?"

She chuckled. "It was more than that and you know it."

Just then the waitress appeared with their colas, promising their food would be ready shortly.

She reached for the drink. "You stepped in to help. You were as concerned about the waiters as you were for the owner. But, more importantly, you seemed to accomplish more in a few hours than most people do in a few weeks or even months."

"I could say the same for you."

"That I talk a lot on the phone," she teased.

"Touché. I meant it's fascinating watching you work. At the spec house, you walked in, you saw a problem, and you fixed it. And fixed it well."

Chuckling softly, she grabbed a fork and fiddled with it as she spoke. "You cannot compare redecorating a little with saving a man's business and keeping a slew of people from the unemployment line."

"I don't know. It shows that maybe we're not very different."

Her brows knit together the same as they had a moment ago.

"It was pretty obvious you love what you do."

"Most of the time."

"Uh, oh. That doesn't sound good."

"Well." She blew out a sigh. "I love what I do, but some clients are very frustrating."

He reached for a spoon and fiddled it between his fingers. "Remind me to keep you away from the people who work with me."

That had her laughing, he was happy to see it.

She shook her head. "I have this one client. The man's new wife hasn't got the design sense of a spider building a web. She wants to take a grand old house and turn it into a new century modern mess, mostly in purple."

"Purple?" Not one of his favorite colors. For the next few minutes, she shared her frustrations with the trophy wife, her lousy taste, and all while trying a new venture in Houston.

"That's why you're here?"

"I love working in Dallas. It's a great city. But I miss not being closer to Emily. Her business degree brought her to Houston and my art degree took me to Dallas. Emily happily bought a cute little house in an equally adorable suburban neighborhood and I gravitated to a loft in Uptown with all the other under thirty Dallasites."

"Not to mention the nightlife."

"Bingo." Her smile held a hint of all the fun he suspected she'd had through the years. "But, as the years go by, and adulting gets busier and more complex, it's harder and harder for either of us to make time for the drive, and I've grown tired of waiting for them to do something about the proposed bullet train."

"You're not the only one tired of waiting."

At that moment, the waitress reappeared with two plates. Setting a plate in front of each of them, she straightened and smiled at them. "Will you be needing anything else?"

Liz snatched a still hot chip and glancing at the condiments to her left, nodded. "I'd love a little mayonnaise, please."

Lifting the warm burger bun, Devlin glanced at the still sizzling burger. He'd forgotten how delicious these burgers were. It had been eons since he'd been here. Lifting his head, he smiled at the waitress. "Looks perfect."

As soon as the woman walked away to tend to another customer, Liz bit into her burger and Devlin would have sworn her eyes almost rolled back into her head. "I know these are good, but they're better than I remember."

Lifting the massive burger to his mouth, Dev took a bite. She was right. He had forgotten how good the fire-grilled burgers that were actually still bigger than the bun tasted.

"So," Devlin set his burger down on the plate, "tell me more about this Houston venture."

"I've got an opportunity to expand my business into Houston."

"Which would bring you closer to your sister?"

She shrugged. "If it works out. I just don't know if I'd be spreading myself too thin."

As she explained, he nibbled on his chips and realized that the more he heard, the more he hoped it worked out for her. What he didn't know was if he wanted her here for Emily, or for himself?

CHAPTER EIGHT

"Let me make it up to you?" Devlin pulled the car to the curb in front of the home where Liz was staying with her sister.

"There's nothing to make up. I had a very nice—different, but nice—evening." Nothing had turned out the way she'd expected, and she certainly hadn't needed the cute black dress to hang out at the hospital or eat a burger, but that didn't matter at all. Watching Devlin Baron in action had been absolutely fascinating. Even though her sister had talked about the man and his projects and charities and all sorts of things for years, it didn't feel truly real until now. Whatever her mind thought a wealthy man would be like, this was not what she'd conjured up. Somehow, she'd always thought arrogance, indifference, and even a hint of narcissism came with money and power.

If Devlin had a millionaire sized ego, she didn't see it. All the man wanted to do was to help. He'd been truly worried about all the people out of work and for the restaurant owner.

"I can think of a lot of women who would disagree with you." Not waiting for her response, he stepped out of the car and circled the hood, quickly opening her door.

Liz accepted the proffered hand, and sliding around, she stepped out of the car and stood in front of Devlin. "I'm not like most women."

"I've noticed."

Her cheeks pulled with a smile. She certainly hoped that was a compliment. "Thank you for a very nice evening."

"If I can't make it up to you, at least let me try for another dinner?" He wasn't moving.

Throwing her arms up, she chuckled. "Who am I to argue, if you insist."

"I insist." He took a step in retreat. "How about tomorrow night?"

"Sunday?"

"You don't eat on Sundays?" He smiled at her.

"Well, yes, but don't you Barons have a big family dinner on Sundays?"

His brows rose high on his forehead.

"Emily may have mentioned something about that a time or two."

"Ah." He nodded. "Yes, whenever possible, many of us show up at the ranch for Sunday dinner, but I can skip a Sunday or two."

"Then I guess tomorrow will be fine. Thank you."

Falling into step beside her, he nodded. "Great. I'll pick you up at six?"

"Sounds good."

Before they reached the front door, Emily opened it and arms crossed, tapped her foot. "For what it's worth, I was about five minutes shy of calling Houston PD. Don't either of you answer your phones anymore?"

Liz pulled hers out of her purse. "Dead. Sorry."

His phone in his hand as well, Devlin sighed. "I put mine on silent at the hospital and forgot to turn the sound back on when we left."

"Hospital?" Emily's voice rose an octave.

"We're all fine." Liz turned to Devlin. "Thank you again. I'll update my baby sister and see you tomorrow."

"Fair enough." Devlin gave her a lazy salute, then faced Emily. "Sorry about the phone."

Emily nodded and smiled at him and as soon as he rounded the hood to the driver side of his car, she closed the door. "Considering it's two o'clock in the morning, that must have been one heckuva *not* date."

"If anything ever qualified as not being a date, this was probably it." Kicking off her shoes, Liz marched into the kitchen and pulled out a wine glass and showed it to her sister. Emily nodded and Liz pulled out a second glass, then poured.

Seated on the sofa with a glass of Pinot in hand, Emily looked at the swirling glass a moment before leveling her gaze with her sister's. "I'm listening."

"He really is nice," were the first words out of Liz's mouth.

"He is."

"I mean really nice."

Emily tipped her head to one side. "What happened?"

"Dinner didn't go as planned. First, Devlin got called to the spec house because someone set off the alarm."

"Anything serious?"

"Nothing was taken so either it was stupid kids or buyers too impatient to wait for a realtor."

"Ha. I'm going with the first option."

"Anyhow, when we got to the Steer's Den, the place was on fire."

"Oh, my lord. Stuart?"

"Is fine. Minor burns, but Devlin went to the hospital anyway." Taking a slow sip of wine, she sighed. "He was really worried about everyone. By the time we left the hospital, not only had Devlin made sure that everyone was being taken care of, that everyone's bills were covered, but he managed to secure a new restaurant location for Stuart."

Bobbing her head, Emily smiled. "That sounds about right."

"Is he always like that?"

"Like what?"

"A hurricane. In reverse."

"I don't think I've ever heard of such a thing."

"A hurricane flies through at insane speeds and destroys everything in its path. Devlin came through with the same gale force winds but instead of destruction, he put all the pieces back together."

"In the right hands, money and determination can do that."

"So this is, like, normal for him?"

"For all of them."

"All?"

"The Barons were born learning how to make a

difference." Emily set her glass down. "If you've been at the hospital all this time, you must be starved."

"No." Liz grabbed her sister's arm before she could stand. "We stopped for a burger at Kelly's."

"And you didn't bring me one!" Despite the teasing tone, Liz knew her sister was serious.

"Sorry. Thought you'd be asleep by the time we got home."

Leaning back in the sofa again, Emily picked up her glass. "So, tomorrow?"

"He wants to do dinner again. I told him he didn't have to, but he seems to be a bit stubborn."

Emily almost choked on the sip of wine she swallowed. "Understatement, meet Devlin Baron."

The entire night felt awfully surreal, but she couldn't help but wonder, what the heck would Mr. Understatement Baron have in store for tomorrow?

Normally, at this hour of the night, Devlin would have gone home to his own apartment for a reasonable night's sleep. Tonight, or more accurately, this morning, he opted to head to the ranch instead. Liz had been right about one thing, Sundays were important to his family. Especially his grandmother. If he was going to skip out on dinner, at least he could do lunch, and sleeping at the ranch would allow him to avoid waking up at the crack of dawn to make it.

The entire drive to the ranch, his mind ran through his evening. A list of things to follow up on Monday morning for Stuart should have been the priority, but every few moments his mind would wander off to Liz. The vision of her in the doorway Friday night in that form-fitting black dress took turns with her digging into the Kelly burger with gusto. Usually, he had people figured out pretty quickly. That's how he made deals work, and work fast. Reading people came easily to him, knowing when to push and when to pull back. Not with Liz. The woman he met Friday night was bold, confident, a bit of a tease, and seriously sexy.

That alone was confounding. How could two women look so much alike and tug such different reactions from him? One he adored the same way he adored his own sisters and cousins. The other had his nerve endings jumpy and his blood sizzling. Fast forward to tonight, or last night depending on how you looked at it, and that same daring woman from the gala was quiet, respectful, patient, concerned, and still driving him crazy.

Leaving his car parked in the circle drive, he trotted up the front steps and into the house. Too wound up to sleep, he made his way to the family parlor. Maybe a short drink would help wipe Liz out of his mind long enough to get some sleep.

"Don't you look like a man wrestling a bull."

Devlin looked down at his shirt.

"I don't mean physically, I mean in your mind. If your frown were any deeper someone could ride a canoe down it." His cousin Porter tossed his book aside. "Want to talk about it?"

"All is well." Devlin poured himself two fingers of bourbon neat. "What has you up at this hour?"

Porter rolled his eyes. "Dropping chaff."

"Look at you. The contractor using military pilot lingo." Devlin dropped into the armchair closest to his cousin. "Hey, legitimate question. What *are* you doing here reading alone after two in the morning?"

"I rest my case."

"There is no case. There is no wrestling bulls, but you are awake in the middle of the night. Going to tell me what's up?" He bit back a smile. Devlin loved his cousins as much as his siblings, but some of them were more fun for verbal sparring than others. Porter was definitely one of them.

Shaking his head, Porter flashed a lazy smile. "Actually, the book turned out to be better than I expected. My mantra for the night seems to have been one more chapter. Now you tell me, what's going on in that head of yours?"

"The Steer's Den caught fire tonight."

"Anyone hurt?"

"Nothing serious."

"And the building?"

"A total loss."

Porter hissed. Now he had a frown deep enough for a canoe to float down.

"I've made arrangements for him to use the space at the Quadrangle."

"Good call. I'll call Stuart tomorrow and see what we need to do for his operation."

Devlin figured his cousin would be willing to help. The whole family dined at Stuart's with some regularity, there was little doubt everyone would want to help if they could.

"So what's with the smile?"

"Smile?"

"Are we going to do this verbal dance again? That frown switched to a smile and it's not a glad to help smile. Who has you smiling?"

"Why does it have to be a who?"

"I've seen your we're-going-to-make-a-killing-on-this-deal smile and that's not it. It looks more like you've found yourself some tantalizing—"

"Careful."

"Again, I rest my case."

Why was he bothering. "I had dinner with Emily's sister."

Porter's brows rose high. "Sister?"

"Yes, sister."

"Now that's interesting."

"Watch it."

Hands up, palms out, Porter shook his head. "Sorry. I always thought you and Emily would wind up together some day."

"Why does everyone have such a hard time believing we're just good friends? Eve didn't wind up with Jack."

"Touché. But the sister?"

"Haven't quite got her figured out."

"She's a woman. Figuring her out is unlikely."

Maybe. But one thing was sure, he was looking forward to trying.

CHAPTER NINE

If Liz had a hard time deciding what to wear last night, today wasn't proving to be any easier. Especially on only a few hours' sleep. When Emily started yawning after every other sentence, Liz feigned being tired too and they both went off to bed, except Liz spent more hours thinking of Devlin than she finally did sleeping.

Standing in front of her sister's closet, the sound of her cell phone ringing startled her out of her thoughts. Spinning about, she hurried to where she'd set her cell down and snatched it up. "Hello."

"Hi." There was no need for introductions. After only two evenings together, she recognized the voice that warmed her through the phone line.

"Hi." If Devlin needed more words, he was plum out of luck. Right now her brain wasn't capable of coming up with something brilliant to say.

"Listen."

Her heart stuttered and her eyes slowly closed as she braced herself for the cancellation of their dinner date.

"I was thinking we should do something besides eat."

Not what she expected, but he most definitely had her interest. "Like what?"

"No, ma'am. It's a surprise, but wear comfortable clothes."

"Comfortable? As in sweatpants, jeans, or my bathing suit?"

"Bathing suit," the words came out so low they almost weren't audible. On top of that, she wasn't totally sure, but she thought she heard him sigh. "That might be a little too comfortable. Jeans or sweats or something else is up to you."

"Up to me. Got it. All right."

"I'm also going to pick you up a little earlier if that works?"

"How earlier?"

"Is four o'clock okay?"

Her gaze darted to the clock on the nightstand. No time for shopping, but enough time to make herself presentable. Actually, she wanted a lot more than presentable, she was hoping for knock his socks off. "I can do that."

"Great. See you then."

"See you." She swiped her phone to end the call and her sister walked into the room.

"What did you decide to wear?"

"I haven't. Devlin just called. He said to wear comfortable." She lifted her eyes to meet her sister's gaze. "How do you dress comfortably for a billionaire?"

Emily stepped closer. "What time is he coming?"

"Four."

"Then he really does mean comfortable." Emily stepped past her and pulled out a handful of clothing dangling from hangers and spread them out on the bed. About thirty minutes later she'd settled on a pair of black Capri pants that gently hugged her hips and a cobalt blue, three-quarter sleeve top with a splattering of small flowers with sparkling centers. Thirty minutes after that, she and Emily had found the perfect rubber sole sandals to go with it, and an hour and a half later she was climbing into Devlin's car.

"Where are we going?" She clicked the seatbelt latch in place.

"You'll see." Repeating almost verbatim what she'd said to him last night, his lips tipped up in a teasing smile.

"Payback?"

"I prefer to think of it as returning the favor."

What the heck was he thinking? Another burger joint? That would certainly explain his not wanting her to wear another black dress. Not that anyone cared that she'd walked into one of the oldest burger joints in Houston dressed for a night of champagne and caviar.

Just outside the loop near a newer suburban development, Devlin slowed. When the car turned into a nearby parking lot, Liz glanced up at the sign—Top of the Putt. Miniature golf?

"Don't look so excited," he teased.

Opening her eyes wide to remove any frowns and wrinkles, she smiled at him. "I don't think I've played putt putt golf since I was a little girl."

"Did you like it then?" He pulled into a parking spot.

Actually, she'd loved it. To this day she wasn't sure if Uncle Fred had intentionally let her win, or if she'd actually bested her mother's brother, but she had enjoyed it. "If memory serves me correctly, I was pretty good at it."

"Really?" He unsnapped his seatbelt.

She bobbed her head. "Really. And you?"

"My family enjoys competition on all levels. My brother Kyle has a friend who owns a few courses and every so often a few of us will pop over and see who's king of the greens."

"King of the greens?" She chuckled. "Is this one of his putt putt courses? The friend?"

"No. But it's a nice one and not too far from Emily's." Stepping out of the car, he met her by the passenger door and extended his elbow to her. "Shall we?"

The closer they got to the actual course, she was able to recognize the theme. "This is Wonders of the World."

Dev's head bobbed. "The owner got the idea from an old movie."

"*Overboard*."

"You like old movies?"

"I like that one." Though the place seemed way bigger and much more impressive than the course in the movie. Inside the main building that led to the actual course, her gaze darted over to the arcade room. Now that was something she wouldn't mind a crack at.

Devlin got an enormous kick out of Liz's reactions. Expressive eyes gave away her thoughts as clearly as a glass window. First when she spotted the sign for the miniature golf course, then again when she recognized the theme for the course, and again when she spotted the arcade section of the business. Everything about spending time with her was proving to be a sheer delight. "Ready?"

"You better believe it." Her fingers gripped tightly around the golf club, Liz stood in front of the first hole, a replica of the Taj Mahal. Swinging the club slowly, right then left, her hips followed the motion sending the small ball down the side of the miniature pool and into the mouth of the famous monument. "I believe," she grinned, "that would be a hole in one."

He didn't say a word, stood where she stood, studied the path to the monument, tested the weight of the club, eyed the path one more time for good measure, and slowly swung. The ball followed the same track as Liz's ball and sailed into the mouth as smoothly as her ball had. Holding back on the grin that wanted to take over his face, he straightened and turned to her. "Shall we move on?"

For the next few holes, he watched her go through the same ritual, doing his best to ignore the cute way she wiggled her hips with each swing, as if that would somehow help the ball's momentum. Coming up on the Great Wall of China, they were neck and neck and the playful tension was growing. The way she'd sway her hips, swing the club, then smile at him and do it all over again, it finally dawned on him that Liz was as competitive as anyone in his family. More importantly, she was going through all those motions merely to distract him from his game. The little stinker. It took everything in him not to laugh out loud. He'd been had. "When did you say was the last time you played?"

Her head tipped to one side and her gaze landed on him. "A long time. Apparently, it's like riding a bike. You don't forget."

"Were you this good a *long time* ago?"

She shrugged, then smiled. "Better."

The twinkle in her eye whenever she smiled got him

every time, but that didn't mean he didn't want to beat the pants off her, so to speak. "Better, huh?"

Hefting a shoulder in another shrug, she smiled coyly. "Am I going to have to give you a handicap?"

"Handicap?" Oh, that did it. "Not on your life." Stepping up for his turn, he squatted down, studied the layout, and pushing to his feet, he gripped the club firmly and gently knocked the ball in the right direction. Resisting the urge to do something silly and stupid like pretend to blow at the ball for it to go in the right direction, he stood straight and held his breath. The ball slipped into the designated hole and his arms shot up at the same second he happily shouted, "Yes!" Doing a fist pump and refraining from adding in a small jig, he spun around and smiled back at her. "I could, of course, give you a handicap if you'd like."

"Ha," she scoffed, and swinging her club at her side, she waved him on with the other arm. "Shall we continue?"

At the last hole, they'd been toggling back and forth with lead score. Devlin had no idea who was going to win. With steady confidence, Liz walked up to the next tee and in a quick move, sent her ball straight for the hole. When it swerved around instead of sliding in, she was as surprised as he was. "Well, foo." On a sigh, she walked up and tapped the ball into the designated hole before slowly turning to face him, forcing a smile. "All yours."

Only one stroke and Devlin accomplished what Liz had not, he was now ahead of her. Somehow, winning within his grasp wasn't as rewarding as it usually was. He wasn't ready to win, to end the interaction, or to gloat over his accomplishment. "Care to go for double or nothing?"

"We didn't bet."

"Not too late." Playfully, he wiggled his brows at her.

Momentarily biting back a grin, her gaze shifted to the main building. "How about a change of pace?"

"How much of a change?"

"The arcade?"

Determined not to smile widely, he shrugged. "Works for me." Especially since he and his siblings and cousins were pinball stars. He dared to place his hand on the small of her back and guide them forward. Maneuvering through the crowd of teens and families, they crossed into the arcade area of the entertainment center.

Without hesitation, Liz marched forward, stopping in front of her game of choice.

"Skee ball?"

She nodded.

"Wouldn't you rather test out one of the pinball machines?"

Dropping one hand on her hip and lifting a single brow as she stared at him, she didn't say a word.

"I guess not. Okay. Skee ball it is." After all, how hard can it be to toss a medium-sized ball into a big hole?

At first, she seemed to take it easy on him. Only landing her balls in the center forty point spot. Each time she handed the turn over to Devlin, she'd smile. Except after the first few turns, that sparkle in her eye sharpened and he just knew he was in trouble.

Sure enough, her next turn, she stood low to the table and the next thing he knew the ball landed in the upper corner with the 100-point hole. Sucking in a deep breath, he stood where she'd stood, stared at the destination and willed the ball to do what he wanted. Instead it bounced over and rolled around then sank into the twenty-point hole.

"Want some tips?"

He shook his head. "I'll find my rhythm."

Liz shrugged and her next few turns, once again, landed in the high score slot. The woman clearly had a golden arm, and he wasn't the only one to notice. A small crowd had formed behind them. Every time she landed the top point spot, the growing crowd erupted in cheers or applause. The odd thing, anyone else, any other time, and his Baron competitive streak would kick in. In his younger days, he might even have been annoyed that she was not only beating him, but garnering all the attention. Not tonight. Right now, a slow grin tugged at one side of his mouth. He was actually proud of her performance. An overwhelming urge to growl at a few of the guys eyeing her with a little too much interest and shout at them to back off, the girl was his. Just one problem. The girl wasn't his. The girl was the twin sister of one of his dearest and most important friends, and as well as he knew Emily, he had no idea what she would say if she knew that Devlin was most definitely smitten with her sister.

It was time for the last ball of the game. No way Devlin could come even close to beating her, and he didn't care. Holy cow. He didn't care. How was that for a first? She stood in the same spot as always, winked at Devlin, and then tossed the ball up the board and into the designated hole. The group that had grown even larger cheered. There was little point in Devlin continuing to play, she had won handily, but as she stepped aside and waved him up for his turn, he smiled at her and took the ball. Almost with no concern or planning, he tossed the ball and to his surprise, the thing bopped up and into the 100-point hole. How about that?

Another second and Liz had flung herself at him, wrapping her arms around him and cheering in his ear. "You did it."

Unable to resist, he wrapped his arms around her waist and enjoyed the moment of exuberance. How special was she? Not reveling in her victory, but delighted in his final accomplishment.

Liz inched back and smiling, took another step in retreat.

As if sucker punched in the gut by a heavyweight champ, Devlin was not a believer in love at first, second, or third sight, but right about now, he was most certainly in big trouble. Believer or not, there was no doubt in his mind that he was most definitely falling for Emily's sister, and that scared the hell out of him.

CHAPTER TEN

"I don't think that will work at all." Liz had spent the better part of the last few days trying to gather sources for this make or break project. It had taken her years to develop a stable of reliable—quality—sources. Why she'd thought she could just scrounge up the same stable in less than a week in Houston was beyond her. Delusional was the only word that came to mind.

"Like it or not, if you really want to expand outside of Dallas, you may have to let Sid and Glen come down." Her assistant had been pushing for transporting trusted craftsmen to Houston. Thankfully, they were willing to bail her out, but the cost of housing and meals and gas for the drive with all their tools and equipment would undercut the bottom line of the job. "This is do-or-die. You know, like a loss leader. Once you prove you're as good as you say, then you'll have the jobs coming in hand over fist."

"All right. I'm going to keep interviewing and researching, but tell Glen and Sid to pencil me in." She wanted this to work very badly. Ever since she and her sister graduated college, they'd lived in separate towns. It was time to be closer again.

"Done. I got a call from Mr. Belker wanting to know when you'd be ready to show them your ideas on the house?"

The urge to growl surprised her. "Tell him that I'm delayed in Houston but I'm working on them now."

"I'll tell him. Maybe I'll send Mrs. Belker some gourmet chocolate covered strawberries. She seems to have a weakness for specialty anything."

"Great idea. Thanks!"

"This is why you pay me the big bucks," her assistant teased. Heaven knew the woman deserved more money than Liz could pay, but some day when she reached her goals the best assistant she ever had would get a well deserved raise.

A few smaller details out of the way and Liz disconnected the call, returning her attention to the swatches and samples she'd picked for the hotel side project. Hotels weren't her normal clientele, but when the opportunity arose, she couldn't resist. She didn't have ambitions to be rich like the Barons, but she did aspire to grow her business into something that could allow her to splurge on travel and a few of the finer things in life without having to sacrifice an arm or leg, or someday her first-born.

Rich like the Barons. Devlin. All week she'd hoped he'd call her for another date. Hoped that there was more to their few evenings together than an auction agreement or a thank you for services rendered. Dinner had been wonderful. They'd stopped at a mom and pop Italian restaurant. Not flashy, but cute, and the food was amazing. She'd probably eaten enough stuffed mushrooms for half the patrons. The conversation had been easy, comfortable, and fluid. When he'd dropped her off at Emily's door Sunday after dinner, she'd thought for a moment, the way he seemed to lean, that maybe he was going to kiss her. Instead, he'd inched back, thanked her again, and waited until she'd locked the door behind her to turn and leave. She'd discreetly watched him through the crack in the living room curtain and didn't look away until long after his car had disappeared down the street.

"Any luck?" Emily popped her head in the guest-room door, hesitated a moment, then let herself into the room. "Not going well, huh?"

Since she hadn't shared with her sister how much she'd enjoyed her time with Devlin, or how every time her phone buzzed, she'd snatched it up thinking it might be him, or how her stomach sank when another name appeared. "Could be worse."

"Tell little sister all about it." The teasing reference to the seven-minute difference in their ages was Emily's fall back to make Liz laugh. Most of the time it worked too.

"Nothing much to tell."

"Okay. Tell me not much." Emily smiled and now that she had Liz alone, Liz knew there would be no getting out of telling her sister the truth.

"Besides the challenges of putting together a reliable work crew here in Houston, I suppose I have a few other things on my mind as well."

"Other things, or a man?"

Liz's gaze shot up. Why did her sister always have to read her so well?

For most of the week, Emily and her sister had barely crossed paths. Liz had been working day and night on her new Houston ventures and Emily had kept pretty busy herself at work. Still, Emily had known in her gut something was bothering Liz and now she could see there was more to it than finding a crew. Some things never changed and her sister's expression was shouting *man trouble*.

Liz chuckled. "Why do you know me so darn well?"

"What can I say?" Emily shrugged. "Maybe it's because Mom insisted on dressing us alike for the first ten years of our lives."

"Oh yeah, that explains it." Liz laughed loudly.

"So who is it?" Even though Emily was pretty sure she knew. Every time she talked to Devlin this week, he sounded off. Not his normal confident self. The man never hemmed or hawed, and yet, every time they spoke, he seemed to be searching for words. A few times he managed to casually slip in asking about Liz, but Emily was pretty sure there was nothing casual about it. From the look on her sister's face now, betting that the two of them had taken a fancy to each other would not be gambling.

Her sister blew out a sigh. "I thought Devlin had a nice time the other night."

Emily didn't say a word, but she knew it was going to be Devlin on her sister's mind. "It sounds like you both had a good time."

Liz nodded. "That's what I thought, but I guess he was just being nice to your sister."

While Devlin was a nice guy who would most definitely want to be kind to family and friends, Emily doubted he was merely being altruistic. Debating what to say next, how not to betray what she knew about her dearest friend, but still wanting to make her sister feel better, Emily couldn't make up her mind. About to reassure her sister that Devlin had clearly been out of sorts all week and Emily's money was on Liz as the reason, she didn't get the chance. Liz's phone rang and the second her glum expression fell away, Emily knew who was calling. *Devlin.*

For the better part of the week, Devlin had done his best to stay focused on business. No matter how hard he pushed, no matter what business he dived into, Liz kept creeping into his thoughts. Her smile, her sense of humor, and those deep blue eyes that could mesmerize him with the simple blink of her lids.

Though the idea was absurd, somehow he felt like falling for his best friend's identical twin was akin to being unfaithful to Emily. The feeling made no sense at all since they were not now, nor had they ever been an item. She truly was his best friend. Always bringing balance to his perspective, always protecting him from the cloying gold diggers only interested in the Baron fortune and his access to it, and always making him laugh when life got a little too intense.

The problem, of course, was that he couldn't shake off the way he felt about Liz, so after picking up his cell multiple times over the course of the day, this time he hit call and waited for Liz to answer.

"Hi," her voice sounded soft and quiet and a little low.

"Hey." Swallowing, he pushed to his feet and began pacing as he spoke. "Are you busy?"

"Just working. Nothing that can't wait." Her voice sounded stronger.

"Have you ever been horseback riding?"

"You mean sit on a horse as it follows butt to butt with more horses on a trail? Not since my eighth-grade graduation trip to a dude ranch."

He couldn't help but chuckle. "I was thinking something a little less regimented. At the ranch. Tomorrow. If you're free."

"The ranch?"

"My grandparents' home."

"Ah."

He wished he knew what she was thinking. "Is that a great idea *ah,* or a how do I get out of this *ah*?"

There was a hesitation just long enough to make his palms sweat. For most of his life, asking a woman out wasn't a challenge—after all, who didn't want to date a Baron? Not till this moment did he realize how much he'd taken that for granted.

"Liz?"

"Sorry. Yes." She chuckled softly. "I'd enjoy that. I think."

"Wonderful." He hadn't really thought through much more than calling Liz to hear her voice. The invitation to the ranch just sort of slipped out. Now he was glad it had. "How about I pick you up around one o'clock?"

"I have some errands to run in the morning. How about I meet you at the ranch around two? Will that work?"

"Whatever the lady wants. Oh. Is your sister around?"

She hesitated before finally answering. "Yes. She's right here."

"Would Emily like to join us?" Having Emily along would allow him to see how she reacted to the two of them. Not that Liz and him were an item, but if Emily was okay with their budding friendship, maybe, just maybe, anything was possible.

Another long moment of hesitation. No doubt Liz had

put her phone on mute and was now talking to her sister.

Finally, Liz's voice popped back. "Can she play it by ear?"

"If I can play hooky from existing plans, I will," Emily called out. "Fair enough?"

"Fair enough." At least Liz had agreed. For the first time all week, his heart wasn't heavy and he felt like smiling. Oh, heck was he in trouble.

CHAPTER ELEVEN

Why Devlin had bothered going to bed last night was beyond him. Ever since Liz had agreed to come to the ranch today, all he could think about was how to make the day special. Though, he did wonder what was he thinking subjecting her to his matchmaking grandparents. Punching his pillow every half hour or so, he'd considered changing the plans. Perhaps finding somewhere else to take her riding. Heaven knows he had plenty of friends with ranches with horses. Heck, if he called their neighbor Jared who'd married his cousin Eve, there was little doubt that Devlin would be able to take Liz out for the day without concerns for what his family would say.

Then again, over burgers, he'd promised her a family dinner after raving about Hazel their cook, who was as much a part of the family as housekeeper Alice on the Brady Bunch. No matter how he sliced it, his grandparents were going to meet Liz, so in the end, he decided to go with the flow and bite the bullet, so to speak. Especially if what he was feeling and thinking about Liz was more than a passing infatuation. Oh, how he hoped Emily was okay with the possibilities.

Tinkering with some numbers on his computer, he tried not to keep looking at the clock. Liz said she'd arrive at two. It was still only one forty-five and accepting that he had no idea what numbers he'd already looked at, he slammed his computer shut and slid it into the briefcase at this side. Pushing to his feet, he walked to the front window, careful to stand out of line of sight, he watched the empty drive that led to the main road.

Calling down to the barn, he wanted to double-check for the umpteenth time that the two horses were ready.

"How many times are you going to call and harass Mack about the horses?" Mitch's tone was stern, but Devlin could hear the teasing in his voice.

"Sorry. I'm just crossing my Ts and dotting my Is."

"Which is why you make the big bucks in real estate. So, who is this second horse for anyhow?"

"Emily's sister is coming over. She hasn't been on a horse since she was a kid."

"Are we supposed to have three horses?"

"No. Emily has something else going on, she might join us for dinner."

"Got it." The hint of confusion in Mitch's voice shifted to a humorous tone. "Don't want to tick off Emily."

Good grief. What kind of idiot was he? Here he was spending time with Emily's sister and he still hadn't said a word to Emily about how he was feeling. Heck, how could he, he wasn't sure himself what he was feeling.

"Yoo hoo. Still with me?" Mitch's voice shifted back to something that was neither concern nor humor.

"Sorry. Thinking."

"About the sister?" Now the tone was more serious.

"About a lot of things." Dang, his cousin was always too smart for anyone's good. "I have to get going. Thanks for helping with the horses."

"Any time."

Disconnecting the call, he went to check with Hazel on the afternoon snack he'd asked her to pack. A little wine and cheese and crackers. Maybe some fruit. Like Mitch, she told him to stop fussing and pretty much shooed him out of the kitchen. Now he was back at the window staring at the empty driveway. The second he saw dust blowing up in the distance, his heartbeat kicked up. His feet rooted to the floor, he watched as the unfamiliar sedan pulled up behind a row of family cars already parked in the driveway.

Expecting her to already be out of the car, he looked at his watch. Five minutes to two. She didn't want to arrive early, that made him smile. Another couple of minutes and she was out of the car, straightening the hem of her shirt and staring up at the family home. When she glanced back to the driver door, he wondered what was delaying her. Ready to bolt outside and see what was wrong, she slung her purse over her shoulder and slowly moved down the drive.

Her steps were slow and careful. Her gaze drifted from one car to another, up to the house and back to the drive in front of her. When she reached the front steps, she once again stopped and stared up at the house.

Not wanting to startle her, he waited for her to step up and ring the bell. The family butler appeared in the foyer to open the door before Devlin could catch up and wave him off.

"I'm here for Devlin, uh, I mean, Mr. Baron." Her voice sounded so small, not at all the strong self-assured woman he'd been getting to know.

"I've got this, Jeeves."

"Very well, sir." The man bobbed his head and turning, walked away.

"Punctual." He waved her into the house.

"I do my best." Her steps were measured and her grip on her purse was surprisingly tight. He could see the tension in her hands. "I hope it's okay that I wore jeans?"

He tapped his jean-clad thigh. "Best for riding."

"Good." Her head bobbed but her smile seemed a tad shaky for him.

"Hazel has made a little snack for us. It'll just take me a moment to grab the basket and we can head to the barn."

Liz bobbed her head and followed him through the foyer, her gaze briefly darting up the massive stairwell and into the kitchen. A few introductions and pleasantries aside and they were crossing the patio on their way to the barn.

The urge to take hold of her hand was almost stronger than his will to not be pushy or presumptuous. But what bothered him more was Liz's silence. Her gaze seemed to be darting from one side of the property to the other. The sharp, witty, and spunky woman he'd gotten to know seemed to be lost in thought. Right about now, he'd kill to know what was running through her mind.

Holy Moses. She knew the Barons were rich. Everyone knew they were wealthy. After the bachelor auction and the phone calls at the hospital, she'd have to be an idiot not to know they were a substantial family. For years, Liz had heard her sister talk about the galas and fundraisers and parties and cars and boats and everything that went with being an affluent political family. But knowing all this and walking up a driveway longer than her city block to a mansion the size of an apartment building, unexpectedly drove home the Barons could probably afford to use their money for kindling. The more she saw of the house that reminded her of Tara from *Gone with the Wind*, and the further she walked, the more overwhelmed she was, and the more out of place she felt. This wasn't one night of playful pretend, this was every day, twenty-four seven.

"Are you okay?" The basket in one hand, he cocked his head in her direction.

"Fine." Did that sound more like a squeak than a word?

"You're awfully quiet."

"You're awfully rich." Her hand flew to her mouth. She had not meant to say that out loud. "Sorry. I mean… uhm.." she blew out a sigh and for the first time since pulling off the road, her shoulders relaxed. "I don't know what I mean."

It took Devlin several long beats to finally speak up. "I suppose this house is a bit much. I just don't think about it."

That was the whole point, none of them probably thought anything about the money. "Though the Lamborghini is amazing in person."

"That's Kyle's."

"And the Ferrari?"

He squinted. "I think it's Siobhan's, but not sure."

"You're not sure?"

With a chagrined look on his face, he shrugged. "Honestly, I have a lot of siblings and cousins and can't keep up with who drives what."

She bobbed her head. She supposed that made sense, but if her sister or cousin bought a Ferrari, she would most definitely not forget. "They're nice cars."

"As long as my car has wheels, I'm happy."

That tugged the first smile out of her since she'd driven up. That sounded like the man she'd become so fond of that she couldn't get him out of her mind. He was right. So what if one car cost more than a dozen others. It was only money.

"And here we are." He waved her into the barn.

The darn thing was almost as big as the house. That uneasy feeling of being totally out of her element began to slither up her spine again. "I don't know that this is a good idea."

"Don't worry. Molly is as sweet as can be. She's so docile we let skittish kids ride her."

Shaking her head ever so slowly, she hadn't meant horseback riding, she'd meant to say everything. All of it. The ride, the dinner, them.

"Here you go." Devlin stopped at a stall with a beautiful cognac colored horse inside.

"Molly is almost ready, I was just about to put her saddle on." A man Devlin introduced as Mack the foreman, walked the horse out of the stall, stopping right in front of them.

"If you give her this, she'll love you forever." Devlin pulled his hand out of his pocket and dropped a small apple into her hand.

Devlin was right. The horse not only gently nibbled off her hand, when she was done, she nudged Liz with her head and then wiggled her lips as if she were saying thank you.

"Aren't you sweet?" She ran her hand along the horse's jaw. "Do you like going for rides?"

The horse bobbed her head, surprising Liz.

"Oh, my." She chuckled. "Do you think she understood?"

"I don't think," Devlin smiled. "I know."

Why did that man's smile always make her weak in the knees? She'd heard that expression in movies and read it in books for most of her life, but not till she'd met Devlin

Baron did she understand what it meant.

Mack had the other horse saddled and ready to go in just a few minutes and Liz found herself on a horse following Devlin out of the barn and down the hillside.

Wealthy estate or not, the Baron land was gorgeous. The further they went, the more relaxed she felt. This was no different than the dude ranch back in the day. She could definitely do this. On the other side of a nearby fence, the green grass was dotted with black spots. She'd forgotten the Baron ranch was a cattle ranch. This wasn't the first time she'd seen cattle in the distance, but without a freeway and speeding cars, it felt so serene and soothing. She was loving the ride way more than she'd expected.

"How's this look?" Devlin glanced in her direction.

"For what?"

"To stop and have a snack."

She was pretty hungry. She'd been too excited with the invitation to eat a real lunch before coming over. "Looks great."

Another few minutes and the horses were nibbling on the green grass under the tree and a small feast was spread out on a large blanket.

"How'd you get all this food into that small basket?"

"Hazel is not only an amazing cook, she's a miracle worker too. As a kid I'd have sworn Mary Poppins had nothing on Hazel."

Liz chuckled, visions of Hazel pulling lamps out of a carpet bag went a long way to helping her enjoy the day. She reached for a grape before spreading some cheese on a cracker. "Oh, this is good."

"It's port wine cheese. One of the specialty items Paige has added to the winery."

That's right, the Barons also owned a winery as well as hotels and cattle and who knew what else.

"Feeling better?" His hand landed on her free one.

Her gaze dropped to his hand on hers. She loved the heat that ran up her arm and warmed her heart. "I think so."

"You think?" A slight frown etched down his brow.

"Sorry. I *know*. I do feel better. This is just..." she

waved her arm over the blanket covered with light snacks… "perfect."

The frown slid away, and the tension in his shoulders she'd only just noticed fell away as well.

It hadn't occurred to her that he might have been as nervous about today as she was, nor how much he must have worked to make this little ride and picnic special. "Thank you."

Squeezing her hand, he sighed, blinked, and pulled his hand away. "You are most very welcome."

What she was, was confused. But Devlin's easy manner was going a long way to making all of this feel normal. What she didn't know, had no clue about, was if it could ever feel normal enough.

CHAPTER TWELVE

When Devlin realized that Liz's odd behavior was because of the Baron money, he felt like someone had kicked him in the gut. The Baron money and connections had always been a blessing. Well, with the exception of finding people who cared about them and not their money. Today, for the first time ever, he wished that he'd come from an ordinary middle-class family with a two-story house and a fenced-in yard.

When she finally told him what had her behaving oddly, his heart sank. His money and family were as much a part of him as his fingers and toes, and there was little he could do to change any of that. After they'd stopped for Hazel's snack and she'd smiled that it was perfect, he came within an inch of leaning in and kissing her. Of trying to convince her he was no different than any other man regardless of his bank accounts. As much as he hated it, good sense stepped in and he quickly retreated.

As they rode up to the barn, Devlin noticed she climbed off the horse as easily as she'd climbed on. "When did you say was the last time you'd gone riding?"

She patted the horse's neck and handed Mack the reins. "I was ten or eleven. Spent the summer at a dude ranch that had expanded into a summer camp."

"A woman full of surprises."

"Not really." She smiled.

That smile meant everything to him. He could only hope that in time, she'd be as comfortable around the Barons as her sister is. "Word of warning."

Her back stiffened.

"Nothing bad, but my grandfather is a former Marine."

Still apprehensive, tension obvious in her shoulders, she nodded.

"He may come off a bit gruff, but don't let that phase you. He's really a pussycat in his old age."

The way her one brow shot up higher than the other, he doubted she believed him.

"Really. You'll see. Watch how he is with the dogs."

"Dogs?"

"My cousin Kyle gifted them a couple of border collie mix puppies from a shelter and now the two never leave Grams or the Governor's side." From the way the corners of her mouth tipped up, he suspected that meant she liked dogs. Maybe dinner wouldn't be such a bad idea after all.

At the back door, Hazel greeted them by handing Liz a Boston crème tart fresh out of the oven.

Blowing on it before taking a bite, Liz's eyes almost rolled back in her head. "Oh, my. This is amazing."

Hazel beamed. "Traded recipes with a woman I met from Boston. Her family is enjoying sweet southern corn bread."

"I think we got the better end of the deal." Liz took another bite.

Devlin chuckled. "You may not say that once you've tasted Hazel's cornbread."

Her smile firmly planted across her face, Hazel shrugged. "I may have made some cornbread for tonight."

"Oh. Everything tastes better with cornbread." Dev rubbed his hands together enthusiastically.

"Are we having dinner in the kitchen tonight?" Porter came through the kitchen doorway carrying an ice bucket and stopped short in front of Liz and frowned. "New hairstyle?"

Liz shook her head.

"Lose a few pounds? Not that you needed it."

Again she shook her head and a smile teased one side of her mouth.

"Well, it can't be the jeans."

Both Devlin and Liz broke out in full, rolling laughter as Devlin smacked his cousin on the back. "Sorry, Porter.

Meet Liz Carter. Emily's twin sister."

Porter's eyes rounded wide before a smile took over his face. "Sorry about that. Nice to meet you." Glaring at his cousin, he leaned in and softly muttered, "You could have warned me the sister was a twin."

Biting back a laugh, Liz's eyes sparkled with delight. "Now where's the fun in that?"

"Okay." Hazel waved her arms at the Baron grandchildren. "I have work to do. Y'all can debate genetics and family later. For now, everyone out of my kitchen."

"I need more ice." Porter held up the bucket.

"Fine." Hazel nodded, taking the bucket from his hands and lifting her chin towards the door. "You'll get your ice. Now shoo."

They'd made it into the foyer when Grams came down the stairs, one of the dogs at her side. At the sight of Liz, Devlin's grandmother sprouted a broad smile. "What a pleasant surprise. Devlin didn't tell us you'd be joining us. It's always such a pleasure to have you."

"Oh, yes. Well." Liz turned to Devlin and Porter at the same time the doorbell rang.

Porter stepped away from the group and opened the door.

"Sorry, I'm a little late. Somehow I managed to get everything taken care of." Emily smiled at all the faces staring at her.

Her head turning from Liz to Emily, Lila Baron grabbed the newel post at the bottom of the stair. "I may need to call Dr. Rayburn."

Devlin took a step closer and kissed his grandmother on the cheek. "Sorry, Grams. Liz and Emily are twins."

"Twins?" Grams glanced at one, then the other, and slowly bobbed her head. Another moment and her smile returned. "Well, how much more wonderful is it for us. Come along, everyone. I want to see the Governor's face when he meets you both."

Over the next few moments, Devlin would have sacrificed his soul to have had his phone out and the video recording. The chatter in the living room slowly came to a halt as one by one, a family member looked up and spotted not one, but two Emilys. When his grandfather raised his head and spewed his coffee clear across several feet, like a credit card commercial, the moment was priceless. Actually, lately a lot of things around here were priceless.

Liz had no idea if she should laugh with everyone, or turn on her heel and high tail it back to Dallas. The whole day had been insanely surreal. Yes, she knew the Barons had money. Any idiot would know that. But it hadn't dawned on her until today that the Barons had money with a capital M. They probably ran in the same circles as the other billionaires on the *Forbes* list. Heck, for all she knew, they were on the dumb thing!

And yet, if she didn't look at her surroundings, most of the time, Devlin seemed like an ordinary nice guy. Yes, a nice guy with connections, but mostly just… nice.

"It will be a pleasure having both of you join us for dinner." Mrs. Baron nodded and waved toward the dining room. "I have it on good authority that supper will be served shortly."

At the table, Devlin's grandmother seated Emily and Liz on either side of Devlin. The way the older woman kept eyeing Emily and smiling, Liz almost felt as if the lady knew something no one else in the room did.

The sound of chairs scraping across the hardwood floors filled the room. One by one, family members settled in. Liz glanced down at the table setting in front of her and was once again reminded about the capital M in money. If her first instinct was right, she'd bet a year's salary that the silverware before her was sterling. Not that it should matter, right? After all, a fork is a fork.

Not till Jeeves moved around the table pouring water from a silver pitcher did she realize the purpose of the large goblet to her right. As for the other two, she suspected at least one was for wine. But what the heck was the other for?

As the conversation grew around the table, her confusion over the goblets was solved. Apparently, the larger of the two remaining glasses was for red wine and the smaller for white. It had never dawned on her how much she didn't know about how the upper crust lived. And yet, once the conversation got rolling, a plethora of forks and goblets wasn't really a big deal, was it?

"I heard that Steer's Den is having trouble re-opening?" Mitch passed the bread basket to his right.

Devlin practically growled. "Fire department found evidence of arson. Now the insurance company is refusing to pay out until the cause of the fire can be confirmed—"

Bushy brows buckled together, the Governor nearly growled, cutting Devlin off. "And Stuart proven innocent."

On a sigh, Devlin nodded. "I'm afraid so. Stuart is currently their suspect of choice simply because the place was well insured."

"Of course it was well insured." Mitch's wife flipped the palm of her free hand upward. "It's one of the best, if not *the best*, steak house in Houston. Business is always booming. Burning it down makes no sense."

"Gwyneth is right. We need to do something." Colton, Porter's brother, looked to their grandfather.

Celeste, their sister, set her drink down heavily. "Do we know someone at the insurance company?"

Devlin shook his head. "I've already reached out to every contact I know. The guy in charge of this is young and new and out to prove himself."

"Lord spare me from ambitious newbies." Shaking her head, Eve reached for her wine glass.

"Is the only problem money?" Paige directed the question at Devlin.

"For now, yes."

"Then we'll definitely have to do something." Not bothering to look around the table for her family's reactions, Paige stuck her fork in the mashed potatoes and promptly shoved it into her mouth.

"Like what?" Cooper, another cousin she'd seen at the gala last week, looked on with interest.

Through narrowed eyes, Paige briefly stared up at the ceiling before smiling. "Grams?"

"Yes?"

"What's the fastest you ever put a charity gala together?"

His grandmother tightened her lips, glancing up much the same way her granddaughter had just done before nodding her head and smiling. "Ten days. But that was in the day when the only way to send out invitations was via snail mail."

"There you have it." Paige sat back in satisfaction.

"I'm sorry." Cooper waved a spoon at his cousin. "Have what?"

"A way to help Stuart. We'll organize a fundraising gala. And since it did so well last time," she paused to smile at Devlin, "we can do another bachelor auction."

That was not what Devlin wanted to hear. "What is it with you and bachelor auctions?"

"They make a lot—and I mean *a lot*—of money."

"Can't we just get someone to donate a nice little Picasso or Matisse?" Devlin really did not want to deal with another auction and the Barracuda.

"He does have a point." Bless his grandmother. Devlin had no idea what she was going to say, but as long as it got him out of another bachelor auction, he did not care. "Too much of the same too close together won't have the same draw. It also might dilute the interest in next year's bachelor auction if people expect it to be more common place."

Thank you, Grams. "See? So, who has a spare Gauguin they never liked?"

"Don't look at me." Eve waved her hands. "Though I'm sure we could donate the naming rights to some new perfume if it will help."

"I suppose." Paige frowned. "We'd have to move fast to see what we can gather for the auction. I'm sure Stuart needs a flow of cash sooner than later to keep his people employed."

"I suspect," his grandfather raised a finger, "there are a great many patrons of the Steer's Den who would be happy to donate an auction item, or even a little boost."

"If we want to help, a lot of other people probably do too." His grandmother returned her attention to the food on her plate.

"I don't have any Picassos in my closet," Emily chuckled, "but I'd be happy to lend a hand in organizing."

"Me too," Liz happily chimed in.

Rubbing her hands together as though she were outdoors in Alaska, Paige grinned like a fool. "I'd say we have a plan!"

Everyone at the table seemed to be as excited about another fundraiser as Paige. Even Liz and Emily were in the thick of the conversation now bouncing around the table. Ideas overflowed, and for what it was worth, Devlin had a few of his own, including how to spend more time with Miss Elizabeth Carter.

CHAPTER THIRTEEN

As the dinner progressed, Liz had felt more and more at ease. Devlin had been right. The Governor was a bit intimidating at first, but the way his eyes softened whenever he pet Moon, the dog at his side, went a long way to making her less tense. On the other hand, Devlin's grandmother was a sweetheart from the start. She could have made a cat feel at ease in a room full of rockers.

It took past the appetizers and well into the main course to actually taste the delicious meal Hazel had cooked. Liz had been so taken aback by all the silverware at the table that she'd been more intent on watching who used which fork and spoon than on savoring the dinner. At one point, the creamiest and most flavorful mashed potatoes she'd ever had, tickled her taste buds, and her obsession with not making a fool of herself with the wrong silverware slipped far away. Everything was as Devlin had led her to believe. Heaven on a plate. It was all she could do not to moan when she bit into the cornbread. Normally, she didn't even like cornbread, but this, she could eat the whole pan and then some. Though she did notice a minute too late that she'd been the only one to bite into the square of bread. Everyone else would break a small piece off and pop the single morsel into their mouths. She wasn't totally sure, but she suspected that it was not a family quirk but probably a rule straight out of Emily Post.

If she were going to hang out with these people, she might have to study a copy, and not the abridged version either. "How do you do it?" Liz joined her sister by the dessert table.

Adding a crème puff to the plate in her hand, Emily

tipped her head. "Do what?"

"Fit in?"

"I'm sorry." Emily reached for an almond square. "What are you talking about?"

"I didn't know which fork to use."

Emily turned pensive.

"And I don't think I'm supposed to bite the corn bread, am I?"

This time her sister chuckled very softly. "No. Any bread, you break off a bite-size piece, butter it, and put it in your mouth. Never, ever butter the whole thing then break it off. Not many people know or care, but if you're ever having dinner with the King of England, it would behoove you to remember."

"Have you?"

A frown replaced Emily's smile. "Have I what?"

"Have you been to dinner with the Barons and royalty?"

Emily rolled her eyes. "I may be Dev's plus-one a lot of the time, but no, I've never been anywhere near royalty."

"What else would I need to know if I were to spend time with these people?"

"Most of the time, nothing."

"And the rest of the time?"

"There's a cheat sheet Devlin gave me when I went to a political dinner with him at the White House."

"Now that you mention it, I remember that dinner, but never gave any thought to needing a cheat sheet."

"Political protocol can be tricky. When to stand, when not to stand, whose hand to shake and not shake. The hardest for me is always other women."

"What about them?"

"The rules of etiquette dictate that the senior female must extend her hand first. Which is why no one ever offers to shake the Queen of England's hand in receiving line photos and videos."

"They just curtsy."

"The women, yeah. But when you're at an official dinner party, and you're introduced to a woman who may or may not be older than you, it's a crap shoot who goes first.

Last thing you want to do is piss someone off by not extending your hand because you *think* she's older."

"And here I thought it was all fun and frills."

"Did you two save room for ice cream?" Devlin came up between Liz and her sister.

"Don't tell me Hazel makes ice cream too?" At this point, after tasting so much of what Hazel has cooked, Liz wouldn't be surprised by anything the woman made.

Devlin chuckled to himself. "She does, but that wasn't what I had in mind."

"I don't know," Liz blinked. "I ate an awful lot at dinner and I wasn't even that hungry after the afternoon snack."

"I wish I could." Emily sighed. "I am exhausted and have an early day in the morning, but you know that if I didn't, I'd kill for some of Gertie's butter pecan."

"Gertie?" Liz looked to her sister.

Emily shifted to face Devlin. "You were thinking of Alamode, weren't you?"

He nodded. "None other."

"Blast," Emily snapped her fingers, "I wish I could play hooky tomorrow so I could join you tonight. I love Gertie's homemade ice cream."

"Excuse me." Liz spoke more forcefully. "Who is Gertie?"

"Sorry." Emily turned to her sister. "If you were driving by and saw this old building in the middle of a field that looks like a strong wind could blow it over, that would be Alamode. Gertie and her husband have been making homemade ice cream there since before we were born. The woman has to be as old as Methuselah, but their ice cream is the creamiest I've ever had."

"I think it has something to do with straight from the cow milk. The cream just tastes better," Devlin chimed in.

"I bet." Liz had never had truly homemade ice cream and the suggestion suddenly made her feel hungry for something sweet. As if to corroborate her story, her stomach picked that moment to growl. Smiling at Devlin, she placed her hand on her gurgling tummy. "Sounds like I'm in for an evening of ice cream indulgence."

"You're going to love it."

When they pulled up in front of the place, her sister had not exaggerated even an ounce. The next windstorm was bound to knock the old place over. Inside, it looked like it fell out of the space-time continuum bringing the 1950s into the twenty-first century. Seeing Devlin laughing with an older woman she assumed was Gertie, Liz mentally shook her head. This man was an anomaly. As easily as his wealth and power could be intimidating, she couldn't help but love his down to earth charm and warmth. Who cared if he was crazy rich? It was only money. Except for a few minor faux pas, she'd made it through the day unscathed and in the end, actually enjoyed herself. And she enjoyed being with Devlin—a lot. If she put her mind to it, she could learn how to run with the rich and famous. After all, if her sister had learned to fit in with all these high society trappings, why couldn't she?

All evening, a sense of panic kept licking at Devlin's nerves. He'd barely recognized that Liz was quickly proving to not only be special, but was becoming very important to him, yet at the same time he could see any possibilities of a future slipping away. Every time something that reflected the Baron wealth came into view, her eyes almost glazed over.

Desperately, throughout dinner, he'd wanted to take her hand and whisper *we're just ordinary people.* The problem he faced was that ordinary people didn't use sterling flatware, set a formal dinner place, or keep a stable of horses. They did, however, eat ice cream. And that was all he could think of to show her that deep down his world wasn't all that different from hers. He hoped.

"Gertie, I'd like you to meet a friend of mine, Liz Carter, Emily's sister." Devlin smiled at Liz.

"So glad to meet you." The older woman extended her

hand. "You look so much like your sister and yet," the woman put a single finger to her lips before speaking again, "there's something different."

"My mom is the only one who could easily tell us apart as kids. Emily and I always had a blast confusing Dad."

Gertie laughed. "I bet you did."

"Got any recommendations for tonight?" Devlin glanced at the old-fashioned blackboard riddled with words in colored chalk.

"I'm playing around with dark chocolate, coconut and salted caramel. I think it's a winner."

"Salted caramel?" Liz's eyes lit up.

Gertie nodded. "Also have a plain dark chocolate with sea salt, and a caramel with sea salt." She leaned closer to Liz. "That's how we accidentally got the new recipe, I sort of dropped one in the other and couldn't scoop it all out. Added the coconut for the heck of it."

"Like the old commercial for Reese's Peanut Butter Cups!" Liz grinned brightly.

"Yep. That would be it." Gertie lowered her voice again. "But don't tell anyone. It's our little secret."

"Deal." Liz drew an X across her chest with one finger.

Seated at a corner table, Devlin waited for Liz to take her first taste.

Her eyes widened and then closed a moment. "Gertie needs to call this Heavenly Delight. Wow."

"The problem is they all taste that way." He dipped his spoon into the ice cream and scooped out a mouthful. "Here, taste."

Her face crumpled a moment. "Bananas aren't my favorite."

"This tastes just like banana pudding."

"I guess." Cautiously, she gripped the spoon, eyeing the ice cream with mistrust. Even more slowly, she raised the spoon to her lips and took the tiniest of tastes. Pausing, her face crumpled and she seemed to be lost in thought when she took a bigger taste. Her mouth moving, her eyes opened almost as wide as a moment before and a broad smile took over her face. "Okay, that is amazing too!"

They ate in comfortable silence, digging into the cups of ice cream and making silly faces at each other with every bite. When she offered him a taste of hers, he made a big show of rolling his eyes and moaning with delight. Thankfully, that succeeded in making her laugh. He absolutely loved how her eyes lit up when she laughed from deep inside.

"Feeling better?" He swore to himself he wasn't going to say anything, only do his best to show her that he was just a regular guy who happened to have a good deal of money, but he couldn't help himself. He was feeling oddly desperate about possibly losing her before anything good could develop.

"Better?"

"You know, about everything."

She flashed a smile. "Ice cream does have a way of making everything look brighter."

His phone dinged and he glanced down at it.

"Do you need to take that outside?"

He shook his head. "It's Paige. She's already gone to work on the event. Grams and the Governor suggested using the ranch ballroom instead of the country club to save expense, and she's already gotten responses from a handful of Steer Den's best customers that they're in."

"Wow. That's fast."

"Paige has a way of making things happen."

"I have a feeling you all do."

"I suppose."

"I suppose nothing." Her expression softened. "I watched you last week. Just like your cousin, within hours of tragedy, you had wheels turning and plans coming together."

"Thank you. I'd hoped it would be enough, but without the insurance money, even having the new location secured and ready for a restaurant, there is still too much needed to open the doors."

"How long do arson investigations take?"

He shrugged. "I have no idea. I would guess faster when the prime suspect isn't the policy holder."

"You're probably right." She swallowed her last dollop of ice cream and glanced down at her ringing phone. "Oh, foo."

"Need to take it?"

"It's Mr. Belker. The owner of that exquisite old mansion that his teenybopper wife wants to disfigure." She blew out a deep sigh. "Give me a minute to take this."

The phone to her ear, he watched her pace outside the window. Her head kept bobbing, but her facial expression gave nothing away. When she came back and sat down her expression seemed a bit lighter, but not thrilled.

"What did he want?"

"To tell me that they've decided to take a quick trip to Italy. Something about a fashion show in Milan. They won't be back for a few weeks, so that old house has been given a reprieve. Though I'd rather have a stay of execution."

How he wished he could do something to fix her dilemma. Unsure, but willing to take a chance, he let his hand fall gently on hers. When she didn't react, he squeezed it and smiled.

Her face brightened a bit more and she wrapped her fingers around his. "On the upside, this means I have some time to help Paige. Do you think she'd let me?"

Would it be totally inappropriate for him to jump out of his chair and kick his heels up? A few more weeks. Working with Paige—and him. He and his family might wield a lot of power and connections, but only the grace of God could have kept Liz here longer for him to win her over. "I'm sure she, and the rest of my family, will love it."

Even though the truth was, no one would love it more than he would. Now he had all of a few weeks to make her fall for him, all he had to do was figure out how. It wasn't much, but holding her hand seemed as good a start as any. At least he certainly hoped so.

CHAPTER FOURTEEN

"Holy Moses." Her hands on her hips, Liz surveyed the tables across the far wall of the Baron family ballroom. Once she'd gotten over the fact that the family home had its own ballroom, Liz was able to spend more time oohing and aahing over the wonderful donations that had been arriving steadily since Paige got the word out that the Steer's Den was in need of aid. Who knew that many rich people cared about one restaurant owner.

"Impressive, isn't it?" In a pair of jeans and layered shirts, Devlin's grandmother was amazing. Liz had no idea how old the woman actually was, but since most of her grandchildren were in their thirties, and none of their parents had been child brides, Lila Baron had to be at least eighty years old and didn't look a day over sixty-five. Not only did she have limited wrinkles, her posture was so erect, Liz found herself constantly straightening her own shoulders whenever Mrs. Baron walked by as though she had an invisible book on her head.

A small, blue velvet lined box of what looked to be tiny crystal barbells stared up at Liz. For the life of her she could not imagine what the heck were these supposed to be for or why would anyone want to bid on them. Though upon studying the box, she did discover the crystal was Baccarat. Liz might not be rich and famous, but even she recognized the probably enormous price tag that came with anything Baccarat. She fingered the box of crystal barbells. "It's all lovely."

"My mother had a set of knife rests very similar to those. I think we gave them to Andrew as a wedding gift."

With a twinkle in her eyes, Lila Baron smiled at Liz before picking up a box and carrying it across the room to another table.

Liz cast her gaze on the barbells again. *Knife rest.* Somehow that made sense. Especially with a fancy white linen tablecloth at stake, but looking over at the older woman speaking animatedly with one of the family maids, Liz had the distinct feeling that Mrs. Baron knew all along that Liz had no idea what they were and extremely politely informed Liz without making her feel stupid. That's what Emily kept saying good manners were all about. Making the next guy feel comfortable. When everyone knows what is expected of them, no one is uncomfortable. Maybe being rich wasn't about one-upmanship. Maybe it wasn't anything like the movies made it out to be. And better yet, maybe fitting in wouldn't be so hard after all.

"Hey." His boot heels clicking with every step, Devlin crossed the massive room. "I heard you were here today helping. Looks like quite the haul."

"Why in the name of Jehoshaphat would anyone donate this?" Paige came walking in with a raggedy cardboard box in her arms and dropped it on the table nearest the doorway with a thud. "I mean really."

"What?" Liz followed Devlin over to his cousin.

Paige lifted the folded lids, exposing the contents. "Look at this stuff."

Considering what she saw, Liz understood the woman's reaction. Piles of miscellaneous ornaments, tinsel, garland, a few pine cones covered in sprinkles, a couple of sprigs of what she suspected was mistletoe. Pulling one of the sprigs out of the box, she glanced at it. "Maybe it's not a lost cause? Maybe if we hang these around the place, call it Christmas in July, we can coax a few folks into spending more?"

"Why?" Devlin reached for another sprig.

Bobbing her head at Liz, his cousin smiled. "Could work. Maybe getting kissed by strangers will put folks in a better mood?"

Devlin raised one brow at his cousin, but didn't say a word.

"Yeah. You're probably right." Paige sighed. "But you can't blame us girls for trying." Scooping up the box, she turned her back on them and walked way.

It took a second for Liz to realize that she was still holding one of the sprigs. Lifting it into the air, she called out to Paige, but she was already out of earshot. "I guess I can toss it in the trash as easily as she can." Holding it in front of her, she stared at the sprig, a grin tugging at her cheeks. "Unless?"

"Unless what?" Devlin's brows crumpled in confusion.

Raising it a little higher, she stepped closer to him. "Tradition."

His frown remained and her mouth went suddenly dry. Maybe she shouldn't have said anything. Other than hold her hand for a few minutes the other night, Devlin hadn't made another gesture towards her. Maybe he was trying to find a polite way to ease out of the proposition.

Just as she was about to spew out some excuse for her silly proposition, Devlin took a step in her direction.

Her breath caught as he continued moving closer until she could see the rise and fall of his chest with every breath. Dear lord, he was going to kiss her. His head dipped and his warm breath fanning her face, he paused, his gaze locked with hers, scanning her eyes, possibly reading her soul.

She couldn't move, couldn't blink, and then his mouth closed the distance and pressed ever so tenderly against hers. For the first time in her life, she was sure her toes had curled in her shoes.

Too soon, he eased away and taking a single step in retreat, straightened to his full height. A soft smile took over his face. "That was nice."

"It was." She could feel her lips tipping up into a smile. Her first proposition seemed to have worked out. Would it be too forward to suggest they do it again?

Suddenly, his warm smile slipped and his eyes staring over her shoulder narrowed. The soft words "oh, crap" slid from his lips.

Two of her least favorite words in the English language had Liz glancing over her shoulder in the direction Devlin was frowning. One glimpse of the sauntering female and she had to agree. "Oh, crap."

"Do you think she sees you?" Liz nudged Devlin out of the line of sight of the doorway.

Devlin shrugged one shoulder. "I didn't notice her look up from her phone. Maybe not."

"Then you have time to hide." Liz nudged him another step back. Why, even when she was pushing at him, was she so irresistible?

"Hide? Don't be ridiculous. I'm not twelve."

"No." Liz nudged him a bit more forcefully. "But from everything I've heard, she's a royal pain. Maybe if you try out of sight out of mind, she'll tire and go after someone else."

"That's not a bad idea."

"See?" She nudged him again.

"I don't mean the hiding, I mean the finding her someone else to focus on."

"Fine. You think about it from the storage closet."

Before he realized what had happened, Liz shoved him into the small room and didn't quite close the door all the way. Holding onto the knob, he was about to swing it open and argue he did not need to hide when Courtney sauntered straight toward Liz, her smile wide and as phony as her long red nails. Suddenly the idea of hiding, not for self-preservation but for snooping, held more appeal than he'd expected.

"You don't want to give up, do you?" Courtney shifted a large vase from one hip to the other.

"Excuse me?" Glancing toward the closet door, Liz turned her back to where Devlin was hidden and grabbed a nearby box, busying herself with the unpacking.

"When are you going to realize that Devlin has no interest in you? You're not his kind. A man like that needs a woman who can bolster him to new heights."

Liz turned just enough so Devlin could see her face. Her expression shifted from momentarily baffled to what he suspected was slowly increasing irritation. "And you think you're that woman?" Her tone dripped with disbelief, teetering on disdain.

"I'm more woman than even Devlin can handle, but the important thing is that I can handle him."

She was certainly more woman than Devlin ever wanted to handle. Always had been. He often wondered if she'd gone to the Lucretia Borgia school of ambitious women. One thing he was sure of, all Courtney cared about was money and power. Her modus operandi seemed to be when a man richer and more powerful fell for her charms, she'd discard the current poor schnook she'd married and take on the new one. As far as handling him, she'd have to catch him first. Liz had been correct, hiding was the right move.

"At least I'm sure of one thing. Even with all your money, you're quite delusional."

The way Courtney's eyes narrowed and her nostrils flared, Devlin considered bursting out of the closet and scooping Liz to safety. The gold-digging barracuda looked ready to blow her top.

"You simple-minded fool. You have no idea what you're up against, but..." Courtney leaned forward, setting the vase on the table. "As sure as any fool can see this paperweight glass vase by Tiffany is worth at least fifty thousand, Devlin will see you for the gold-digging cretin that you are."

"Pot calling the kettle black?" Liz was practically sneering with delight.

Shaking her head, Courtney eased back. "No man wants hamburger when he can have steak. And I, my dear, am Grade A, prime beef. Once Devlin has had a taste of me, nothing else will do."

Liz shrugged. "The Barons do seem to like cows."

In order not to be heard, Devlin had to slap his hand to his mouth to stop his laughter from resounding through the ballroom. Who else would have the nerve to call Courtney a cow?

"Keep dreaming, Emily. You won't win this one." Courtney took another step back and spun on her heels. When she reached the doorway, she called over her shoulder, "Tell Paige she can thank me later. That vase will bring a pretty penny. Just like me, everyone in the place will be clamoring for it."

Under her breath, Liz muttered something that sounded like what a witch. Or she could have said something stronger. Either way, Liz had it right. "You can come out now. She's gone."

"And stupid. She thought you were Emily." It had taken an enormous amount of self-control not to shove the door fully open and share a rather angry piece of his mind with the barracuda. If she were a man, he most definitely would have been delighted to wipe that smug grin right off her face.

"She's lucky I'm not. Emily probably would have slugged her for some of those comments."

He chuckled softly. Liz had a point. Emily just might have slugged her. Not for offending Emily, but for attacking Devlin. No one with any brains messed with people Emily cared about. From the way Liz continued to stare down the hall, her teeth grinding, he had the distinct feeling that if Courtney had any idea of what was good for her, she'd stay away from both Carter sisters. And, hopefully, him too!

CHAPTER FIFTEEN

Despite the unpleasant encounter at the ranch between herself and the barracuda, the rest of the preparations for the big event had been nothing but fun for Liz, and quite often downright exciting. Some of the items donated by the rich and famous of Houston were simply amazing. The Tiffany vase was indeed worth even more than Courtney had said it was, but it was far from the most exquisite or costly item. An anonymous donor had brought in a wristwatch given to Jackie Kennedy Onassis by her second husband, the Greek billionaire Aristotle. Liz didn't mind admitting she'd ogled the thing for a very long time.

The plans for the fundraiser had been pretty set in stone overall, but the details had changed from hour to hour. Liz was as flexible as the next person when it came to a change of plans, but the Barons had a whirlwind style that allowed for pivoting on a dime, so to speak. As a result, Liz was learning so much more about just how much hard work it was being a patron of anything. Everyone involved in the event, including Paige and Eve, were dressed in the same outfit. Jeans, boots, and a *Save the Steer's Den* t-shirt. While the t-shirts were identical, Liz knew the boots and jeans Paige wore were way more expensive than her bargain buys.

"Holy cow." Eyes wide, Emily, dressed in the same t-shirt and jeans as Liz, spotted the Jackie Kennedy watch. "Who donated this?"

"Anonymous. Isn't it exquisite?"

"And then some."

"Except for his second wife," Devlin strolled up behind

them, "and possibly that watch, the man had awfully gaudy taste."

Liz couldn't resist scanning the man from the tips of his booted feet to the top of his sandy-brown hair, lingering a little longer on sparkling eyes before smiling. One thing was certain, besides having stunning blue eyes she could lose herself in forever, Devlin knew how to wear a pair of jeans.

The guests were beginning to arrive. Liz had never seen so many Stetsons in one place. The silent auction items had been set up on tables along the side wall. The actual items to be in the live auction, like Jackie's watch and the Tiffany vase, were set up on tables for bidders to preview in an area designed for an orchestra. The number of people perusing the goods in both areas gave Liz goosebumps.

Devlin's phone buzzed. "Grams has determined that we underestimated the last-minute attendees. She wants more tables on the veranda."

"From the barn storage?" Emily seemed to know how the Baron household ran as well as any other family member.

"Yep." Devlin nodded. "Mitch and Mack are sending out an all points bulletin for muscle."

"I'm in." Emily pushed the cotton long sleeves up her forearm and grinned.

About to open her mouth to volunteer as well, Liz stopped at Devlin's raised hand.

Stepping into her private space, he placed an all too brief kiss on her lips. "Someone needs to stay here who knows how to answer any questions the guests may have on an item."

On a sigh, Liz nodded. He had a point. "If you still need help after Paige and Eve come back from checking on the wine and food, I'll come out."

"Fair enough." Devlin nodded.

No sooner had he and Emily crossed through the French doors onto the veranda then, a glass of champagne in hand, Courtney of the many names sauntered up beside her. "The vase should have been front and center."

"Like a ten pin," Liz teased. Not sure why she thought the barracuda might have a sense of humor.

The witch glared at her and Liz did her best to stay calm. This woman could tick off Mother Theresa. "A bowling joke. What I should expect from you."

Liz had to wonder if Courtney still thought she was talking to Emily.

"And here I thought it suited you so well." Flashing a forced toothy grin, Liz probably should have sweetened her words with honey instead of vinegar, but she just couldn't help herself.

For a few seconds, the whites of her eyes circled dark brown orbs, Liz expected smoke to come out of Courtney's ears. Instead, grinding her back teeth, she merely gathered her composure and shook her head. "So childish. Proves my point. Devlin needs a real woman."

Visions of this 'real woman' with a black eye crossed Liz's mind, but she didn't dare do anything to upend the carefully arranged event. Instead, she bit her tongue and side stepped her nemesis. "I'd better see if Paige needs any help."

Shaking her head, Courtney gently raised one shoulder in an indifferent shrug.

Silently counting to ten or a thousand, just as Liz passed the barracuda, she tripped over her own two feet. Or did she? Glancing down at the floor in search of some obstacle to have tripped on, the only thing she saw was Courtney's tapping foot in boots that probably cost more than Liz's weekly income. Slowly raising her gaze to meet the witch's, there was no missing the satisfied smirk on her face. The little… "Having a hard time keeping those size ten blocks to yourself?"

Once again, Courtney's eyes widened, her nostrils flared and any second, Liz was sure steam would be coming out of the woman's ears. The woman was way too easy to rile. "I'll have you know I wear a petite size seven. Perfect size for my frame." The woman actually patted the side of her head as if proving some ridiculous point.

She knew she shouldn't have done it. It was truly

childish to follow the philosophy of tit for tat, but when Courtney spun around to saunter away, Liz couldn't help herself. Her size eight boot slipped forward and Courtney went flying over the boot, and unceremoniously face planted on the hardwood floor.

Heaving up onto all fours, Courtney glared at her and suddenly, like staring a snorting bull in the face, the woman grunted and lunged forward.

Two arms wrapped around her knees and yanked her feet out from under her. Oh, hell, what had she started?

"There we go. All set." Brushing his hands together, Devlin surveyed the veranda. The extra tables were in place and Paige, Eve, and their grandmother were quickly helping the staff pretty them up.

"Looks like we'd better buckle up." Staring ahead, Emily bumped the last table over a smidgeon. "Courtney's here and she's marching straight for Liz."

"Liz?" His gaze narrowed as he searched out the two women. "She'd better keep her distance."

Emily cocked her head to one side. "You really do care for Liz, don't you?"

His best friend studied him so intently, discomfort slithered up his spine. "Of course I do. I care for a lot of people. You included."

Shaking her head, Emily rolled her eyes at him. "That's not what I meant and you know it."

The thought of side stepping, or fudging his way out of the answer occurred to him, but there was no point, he had to face the music eventually and now was as good a time as any. His head bobbed. "Quite a bit."

One brow lifted over eyes that shimmered as brightly as Liz's but somehow, had never affected him the way Liz's did. "I thought so."

"And?"

"And what?" Her brow settled back into its rightful

place. She really didn't know what he meant.

"Are you okay with it?"

Her expression softened as her lips tipped up. "I couldn't ask for a better man for my older sister."

The tired old joke between the twins had them both chuckling. Maybe it wasn't that old or that tired.

"I mean it." She stepped back. "If you two work out, I couldn't be happier. You hurt her and I'll slowly break every bone in your… "Uh-oh." Emily slowly maneuvered around him, her gaze focused toward the French doors. "You-know-who appears to have Liz cornered."

"What?" He'd never liked Courtney, but after the other day when she was so rude and insulting to Liz, he not only deplored her, he didn't trust her as far as he could throw an elephant. Following the direction of Emily's gaze, he located the two women just in time to see Liz stumble and right herself. Narrowing his gaze, he zeroed in on Courtney's face. "That…"

"Now, now." Emily patted him on the arm. "Your grandmother has bionic ears."

Shoving his sleeves up his arms, he began his march across the ballroom, muttering to himself, "I have never struck a woman in my life, but they say there's a first time for everything."

Emily scurried up behind him and grabbed his arm just as Courtney face planted. "See? Sis has this under control."

Stopping in place, Devlin pressed his lips together and held back a laugh. "They do say karma's a bitch. At least now I won't have to slug her."

"There you go, saved by the… "Oh hell."

"Oh hell, what?" Devlin spun around again, his gaze landing on what Emily had seen. Her arms around Liz, Courtney had yanked Liz's legs out from under her and now the two women were rolling around on the ground like a couple of troublemakers at the schoolyard. "I'm going to kill her."

"Oh, no you don't." Emily grabbed his arm hard. "This is going to be fun."

"Fun? Have you lost your mind?" Panic was beginning

to make itself at home in the pit of his stomach. "I need to go rescue her."

"Why would you want to rescue Courtney? She deserves everything she has coming."

"Not Courtney. Liz." Her name may have come out a little louder than he'd wanted it to, but Emily had a tight hold on him and he needed to breakaway and save Liz.

The way Emily kicked her head back and laughed— hard—Devlin considered maybe she'd hit her head or something and he hadn't noticed. Only a mad woman would stop him from protecting her sister. "Believe me when I tell you, Liz most definitely does not need saving."

He turned to see where the two women had been rolling around on the floor, and debated if Emily would kill him for shoving her out of his way. Legs and boots were flying up, then down, arms were flailing and just as he was about to drag Emily across the floor if he had to, Liz popped up, grabbed Courtney by the wrist and a second later, Courtney was flat on her back.

"See?" Emily straightened her shoulders, a proud grin on her face.

Another moment, and Liz straddled Courtney, a tight grip on either wrist, she had the woman pinned to the ground, and rather than break it up, a crowd had gathered around the cat fight.

"What is wrong with everyone?" While he couldn't have cared less what happened to Courtney, he didn't trust her not to pull a sneaky move and actually hurt Liz. He couldn't stand the thought of Liz getting injured. "Come on." He waved Emily on. If she followed him or not it was up to her, but he was not letting this fight continue.

"I'm telling you," Emily scrambled to keep up with his large and hurried strides, "Liz is a second-degree brown belt. She doesn't need anyone's help."

Devlin looked back over his shoulder at Emily. "She's a what?"

"You heard me."

The two stuttered to a stop by the pair on the floor. Both women were perfectly still, glaring at each other.

"Need some help?" he asked.

Liz shook her head. "I'm not letting go until this Botox overdosed bimbo promises to behave like a good little girl."

"There she goes stirring things up even more." Emily rolled her eyes skyward and sighed. "Absolutely no filter."

Trying fruitlessly to pull her arms away, Courtney actually growled at Liz.

"See, what did I tell you?" Emily crossed her arms and winked at her sister.

Flat on her back, Courtney looked at Emily then turned her attention to Liz. Her eyes bulged with surprise before a deep frown settled in and she skewered all three of them with an icy glare. "What the heck?"

CHAPTER SIXTEEN

Ever since taking a tumble with the barracuda, all Liz had been waiting for was for the party to end and to sink into a soft comfortable chair. Battling it out with another person had been much easier when she was sixteen and there were mats on the floor.

"I had no idea you were a brown belt." Devlin sidled up beside her.

"You never asked?" her response was more of a question, punctuated with a chuckle.

Standing on the side patio, Devlin glanced around them and pulled her into an embrace.

Without hesitation, her arms found their way around him and her head rested on his shoulder.

"I will say, you scared the bejesus out of me."

Tipping her head back, she glanced up at him. "Why?"

"Well," he shrugged a shoulder, "besides not knowing you were a martial arts star…"

That made her chuckle. Star. She liked that.

"I also had no idea what Courtney's skills were, but more than that, if she played dirty. Which, knowing her more and more, I wouldn't put past her."

"Nah." Her head fell back against his shoulder again. "She fights like a girl."

Devlin's chest rumbled with laughter, then she felt it. His finger gently lifted her chin to face him again.

Their gazes met and she swore if he weren't holding on to her she'd probably melt on the spot. Had any man ever made her feel so safe, and warm, and content with just a simple look?

"This may be way too soon, and if it is, don't run off.

I'll wait for you to catch up to me, but, Elizabeth Carter, like it or not, good or bad timing, I love you."

"You do?" she barely got the words out.

His head bobbed, his finger still gently under her chin.

"As in, gee golly you and your sister are my best friends, or as in, the big L?"

A smile tugged at the corners of his mouth, and his head inched a fraction closer to her. "As in the very big, extra large, L."

"Hmm," she tried to tease, him but couldn't play hard to get. Instead, she raised her arms around his neck and just before pulling him in closer, whispered, "I love you more."

Floating on a cloud, everything about kissing Devlin was beyond perfect. Only the sound of a husky voice clearing his throat broke through the exquisite moment. "Excuse me."

Regretfully, inching away from each other, Liz glanced over at Porter and Colton, the two brothers standing side by side, looking down at their shoes. The sight actually had her chuckling. Two grown men looking like a couple of nervous schoolboys.

"Uh," Porter started, "the last of the guests is gone and Grams wants everyone in the family room to go over the haul."

Liz took another step back, delighted when Devlin's hand slid down and latched onto hers. He didn't want to let go any more than she did.

As everyone made their way back into the house, Liz was surprised at how many cousins either winked at her, smiled at her, or gave her a thumbs up. What the heck was going on? Surely they didn't all know that she and Devlin were now an item?

"I haven't laughed so hard in years." In the family room, Leah handed her husband a drink.

"The woman has been a menace to the male species for as long as I can remember." Kyle shook his head and poured himself a glass of lemonade.

"And here she is." Jared, Eve's husband, pushed to his feet and raised his glass in Liz's direction. "The conquering hero. I strongly suspect every bachelor from here to Timbuktu appreciates you putting the barracuda in her place."

"Doesn't anyone like that woman?" Liz scanned the room.

Several heads moved from side to side and chorused, "No."

"As a matter of fact, dear." Mrs. Baron walked into the room. "I received several donations from both men and women who were absolutely delighted someone finally put Courtney in her place." The woman turned to her grandson-in-law, Jared. "It's not nice to call people names."

Contrite, Jared dipped his chin. "Sorry, ma'am."

Liz did her best to muffle a laugh. If she could ignore their money, these people were just like everyone else, and Lila Baron could have been any mother or grandmother on the planet.

"I'm sorry." Claire, another of Devlin's sisters, plopped into an overstuffed easy chair. "But when I spotted her limping out of the ballroom, I had to bite my cheeks not to yell out a cheer."

"Claire." Lila Baron frowned at her granddaughter.

"Sorry, Grams, but it's true." Claire smiled impishly at the family matriarch.

"I can do y'all one better." Cooper smiled from where he was seated. "It seems the bara...uh...Courtney is slinking away with her tail between her legs. Donna Klein overheard her exclaim that she'd decided to accept an invitation to visit some Contessa in Spain. Something about being better suited to real royalty, not just a name."

"Brother." Craig put his glass on the table. "That woman can't resist getting in one more dig, can she?"

"Well. However you look at it," the Governor finally spoke up, "at least she's out of everyone's hair."

"For now," Emily added. "I have a terrible feeling all of Europe is going to want to send her back sooner than later. No refunds, no exchanges."

The whole room broke into laughter and Liz couldn't help but think her sister was probably right. It might take a few years, but that woman would find a way to come home in triumph, probably showing off a prince or duke for a spouse. At least, Liz had one thing Courtney the barracuda would never have... Devlin.

The entire fundraising afternoon had been a whirlwind. When Courtney went after Liz, Devlin understood the true meaning of the old expression seeing red. He honestly thought he could rip the woman limb from limb no matter how his parents and grandparents had raised him. After that it took all his self-control not to follow Liz around like white on rice. All he could think of was keeping her safe.

Learning Courtney of the many last names had decided to leave the country hadn't been the only good news Devlin had received today. A short while ago, Stuart informed Devlin that the restaurant owner was no longer under suspicion for burning down his own business. The investigation had tracked down the real culprit. A former employee, who'd been fired for dipping into the till, wanted to get even with Stuart for giving him a poor reference, or two. The idiot was lucky no one was seriously injured or worse. At least now the guy would be guaranteed a roof over his head, three square meals a day, and wouldn't be needing references for a very long time.

So distracted by all the unexpected events as well as the rousing success of the auction, Devlin had almost forgotten his surprise.

"So, what's the bottom line?" The Governor looked to his bride of decades.

Comfortably seated in her favorite chair with Honey the dog, as usual, by her side, Grams reached for a stack of papers. "The initial numbers are pretty darn good. Of course, we occasionally have people who couldn't come send funds later, or even folks who were here and didn't win anything decide to spend anyhow, but for now, are you ready?"

Heads nodded.

"Two hundred and seventy-five thousand dollars, give or take a few."

Smiles and cheers erupted.

"Does Stuart know?" Devlin had invited the restaurant owner and family friend to attend and help schmooze his patrons as well as attendees who had never dined at the Steer's Den. Stuart had been his charming self, but once the bidding started, his nerves kicked in and he opted to go put some elbow grease into the new space while waiting for the news.

Grams nodded. "I phoned him myself with the numbers. He was so excited, he couldn't stop thanking us."

"Who knows." Devlin shrugged. "Maybe, if he likes it enough, the temporary move can be permanent."

Cooper glanced his way. "I never did find out where it is. Is it a viable spot?"

"Very. The penthouse restaurant that had been there went belly up two years ago. Great location, lousy management. With all the new development we've been doing in the old design district, it would be an even better spot for him than the building he'd been in."

"Sounds like a win win to me." Coop nodded.

Seated next to him on the sofa, Liz leaned heavily into his shoulder and smiled up at him. "Do you always fix everyone's problems?"

"All I can do is try. Sometimes it works, sometimes not so much." He chuckled. "Once in a blue moon it all blows up in our faces, but those are stories for another day. Today is a day to celebrate. Stuart has the funds to get everyone back on their feet, the arson squad can investigate for as long as they want, but we know Stuart didn't do it for the insurance money. Courtney is probably already packed for a trip across the pond."

"Lord, if she does land a titled husband, she's going to be impossible when she returns."

"*If* she returns." He certainly wouldn't mind if Courtney fell in love with a duke or earl and settled happily into the aristocratic life, leaving all the eligible bachelors in Texas alone. Including his cousins.

The chatter in the room grew an octave as the family rehashed for the umpteenth time how much fun they all had watching Liz take down Courtney.

"Come with me a minute." Devlin took hold of her hand and pushed to his feet.

Outside on the same spot they'd stood earlier, Devlin pulled a key out of his pocket.

"What's this?" Taking the key in her hand, Liz stared at it with curiosity before looking up at him again.

"A little surprise." Lord, he hoped he hadn't made a mistake, but now was no time to start second-guessing himself.

"Surprise?" An amused grin on her lips, her gaze lifted to meet his. "Care to get a little more specific?"

"The house on Swiss Avenue. The one with the young bride who's fond of, was it pink?"

"Purple."

"Right. Purple. Anyhow, I made her husband an offer he couldn't refuse."

Her gaze dropped to the key. "You bought the house that the teenybopper wanted to deface?"

Mentally crossing his fingers, he nodded, "I did."

Her arms flew around his neck. "You are a miracle worker. How did you get them to sell?"

"Ah, can't give away my trade secrets."

She handed him back the key. "Now what?"

"Now." He shoved the key right back at her. "You get to restore the place to its former glory and then we put it on the market."

Again, Liz threw her arms around him and before he could react, planted a kiss smack on his lips. If this was how she reacted every time he made her happy, he was going to have a great time making her happy for a very, very long time.

EPILOGUE

Nothing like a christening to bring a family together. And the Barons had more than their share of family. Over the last few years, one by one, so many of his cousins had, to his grandparents delight, gotten married. A few had even had children. Leah and Cooper each married into a ready-made family. Mitch and Gwyneth had been the first with the birth of little Beth, and now, here they were at the christening of Cooper and Tess' baby boy, James Everret Baron. A nod to Cooper's father and grandfather.

Emily, his cousin Devlin's sister-in-law, stopped and stood smiling at Porter's side. As one of Devlin's best friends and a frequent plus-one, Emily had been around the family so often it was hard to believe she wasn't a Baron. All of which made it so much easier to have her twin sister Liz in the family. "They look so happy."

"Can't argue. They do. Then again, babies will do that to people. Only a ten-pound bundle of fat and diapers and milk-covered faces can have intelligent adults regressing to babbling idiots."

Emily let out a loud rumble of laughter. "That's true too, but I was referring to Devlin and my sister."

Turning his head in the direction she'd been looking, Porter had to agree with Emily on that front as well. His cousin and his new bride were grinning like the Cheshire Cat. When they were smiling at each other, they also linked fingers, or caressed an arm or a cheek or stole a kiss. They looked so in love it was worthy of a Hallmark commercial. Or maybe one for Pepto Bismol.

"Did you hear the latest news?" Emily asked.

"Wedding, baby, or money?" After all, that pretty much

covered the events in the Baron family of late.

"Well, since Devlin and Liz are already married, and making money is like breathing for the Barons, that leaves baby."

He had to think a minute. Who had been acting any differently? Which husband had been fawning more than usual over his beloved wife? His gaze darted from couple to couple, pausing at Devlin and Liz, who were literally moving across the family party as one, and shook his head. Nope. They were just effervescing with that newly wed bloom of two people so in love everyone else was left longing for a soulmate of their own. Porter's gaze landed on Logan and Leah. The man was staring at his wife as if she were a Ming Dynasty vase. Precious, valuable, and irreplaceable. Yep. They were the ones. "Leah."

Emily bobbed her head. "Isn't it wonderful news?"

He had to admit, he'd enjoyed having Beth and now James to bounce around. Especially Beth—who knew babies could be so much fun? As long as he wasn't the one who had to go home and change the diapers or pace the floor in the middle of the night, he was very happy for all of his cousins.

"Hey." Holding hands with his new wife, Devlin strolled over to the corner of the veranda where Porter and Emily had been spying on the family. "Hiding out?"

"More like enjoying the view." Emily smiled at her longtime friend.

Liz hugged her sister before once again holding Devlin's hand. "It's a nice family."

"It is." Emily retained her smile, but Porter thought he detected a little bit of wishful thinking.

If he remembered correctly, Liz and Emily were the only siblings and their parents had retired young to Florida several years ago.

Slowly, Devlin's arm looped around Liz's waist just as her phone buzzed. Holding up a finger, she took a step away.

"Must be important," Porter said to Devlin.

His cousin shrugged and a moment later, Liz hurried back to the group. "We got an offer!"

"An offer?" Porter must have missed something.

"The Swiss Avenue house. First offer has come in and it's almost ten percent over asking, all cash." Liz's smile made the Cheshire Cat look sad.

"I told you people were going to love it!" Devlin scooped Liz into his arms, and grinning down at her as if he were a starving man and she were a prime rib dinner, the heat between them could have melted anyone within a few feet. "You're an amazing designer and excellent stager. We're going to make a killing working together in Houston."

"Teamwork," Liz smiled up at him, her gaze locked with Devlin's and the heat level rose another notch.

Before the public display of affection began again in earnest, Porter spun on his heels. "Here they go again." Smiling at Emily, Porter sighed. "What do you say if we raid the fridge and see what goodies Hazel has ready for everyone?"

Emily glanced at her sister and smiled more widely before turning to Porter. "I think that's a great idea." Playfully, she linked elbows with Porter. "I'm hoping for the Boston Cream Pie."

"Not me." He chuckled. "I want the sour cream blueberry tarts."

"Works for me too." Emily laughed more loudly.

Porter understood Emily was happy for her sister—after all, he loved his cousins like siblings and was delighted to see each and everyone so happy. But every so often, he wondered if the winning streak for love wasn't bound to run out before it was his and his siblings turn to find the love of their lives. Then again, what was so awful about being a bachelor? Taking one look over his shoulder at Liz and Devlin staring into each other's eyes as if they were the only two people in the world, he had to admit, whatever magic ran in the Baron clan, he really didn't want it to run out anytime soon. At least not before love found him.

Enjoy an excerpt from
Sweet Beginnings

Preston Sweet slammed the door of his SUV and slipped his keys into his pocket. Unlike his apartment in town, the front door of the Sweet ranch was never locked. From the near empty drive, it looked like only his brother Carson had beat him home. Every Sunday the driveway would be filled with cars. Tonight would be the first time the house would be bursting with Sweets on a weeknight for no other reason than his mom had called and asked.

The sound of spitting gravel cut off his thoughts. Even with the dust cloud blowing in the thick summer air preventing a clear view of the approaching car, he knew the driver had to be Rachel. His sister was the only person in the family who considered every open road a NASCAR track.

The car came to a screeching halt within a few feet of him, though it felt like inches. She probably should have moved to Hollywood and been a stunt car driver. "Cutting it pretty close don't you think?"

Rachel yanked her overnight bag from the back seat and shook her head at her brother. "Nah. I had plenty of room."

Even though he had just seen her a couple of weeks ago, he scooped her into a warm hug as though it had been forever ago.

"Any idea what this is all about?" she mumbled into his shoulder. The same underlying tinge of tension he'd felt since his mom's cryptic call, could be felt in Rachel's embrace.

He shook his head, and eased back. "I can't decide if

Mom announcing she's getting married would be best case scenario or worst case scenario."

Like a shot, Rachel sprang back. "Mom's getting married? I thought you didn't know what this is all about."

"No. That's not what I meant." He shook his head more forcefully. "I was simply wondering what could be so important that she would call all of us and tell us she needed us home. *Now*. Then it hit me a wedding would be something seriously important. Especially if it were *our* mother getting married again. Once my mind wandered that far, then I couldn't decide if that would be a relief or the beginning of some new kind of hell."

"She's not even dating." Rachel smacked him lightly on the arm and growled her frustration with her big brother. "Why would you even go there?"

"Because the other option was she's dying and I don't want to go there—*ever*."

On a heavy sigh, Rachel nodded. "That would certainly make getting hitched more appealing."

He reached for her bag. "Did you ever think about it?"

"Mom getting married again?"

Moving forward, he bobbed his head.

"Nope." She fell into step beside him. "I just can't picture anyone with Mom except Dad."

"Know what you mean, but still, it has to be pretty lonely some days in this big old house."

"Yeah." She stopped at the porch steps and looked up at the expanse of the old two story home. "But for now, I don't think this is it."

"I hope so. I'm not ready to go there yet. Some day, but not yet." The way his dad had drummed into all their heads since they were old enough to walk, he held the door open for his sister. "And the more I think about this call, the more I'm sure whatever it is, I'm not going to like it either."

"Any word from Garret?" Rachel strolled past him.

"No, and I didn't expect to hear back from him. He warned us there's no cell service where they're camping in Idaho."

"I know." His sister shrugged. "I just thought,

sometimes with technology you never know."

The inside of the house was neat, cozy, welcoming, and quiet.

Rachel paused mid stride. "I'm surprised Mom isn't here waiting for us."

The same thought had crossed Preston's mind. For as long as he could remember, since the day he'd left home for college, the minute his mom heard the rumble of his engine, she was out the door and on the porch waving frantically at him. As a matter of fact, now that he thought about it, everything inside and out seemed unusually quiet.

"Maybe she's helping the hands with something. This is around vaccine time before the big sales."

"Maybe." Without being given direction, he led his sister down the hall to the room she'd shared with her twin Jillian, and dropped the bag on the bed. "I'm going to see if I can find Carson and Mom."

"I saw a light on in the study." Rachel unzipped her bag. "I'm going to take a minute and unpack."

"Don't you usually pack a lot less?"

She shrugged. "Since I'm mostly working from home, I figured no harm in planning to stay a few extra days."

The thought to pack a bag and turn supper into a long weekend had occurred to him as well, but then he decided that might fall in the camp of dramatically over reacting. Maybe he shouldn't have reconsidered. "That'll make Mom happy."

His sister flashed a huge toothy grin. "I know."

"Women," he muttered, laughing to himself. That kid and his other sister had everyone in the family wrapped around their fingers from the day they were born, and he doubted that would ever change.

Retreating down the hall, he turned into his father's domain. Charles Sweet's study hadn't changed much since the days when Preston and his siblings had trotted around on wooden pony sticks with makeshift lassos and pretended to rope everything from the toy horses to the desktop lamp—and each other. In an effort to keep them all in one piece, their father had dutifully uttered the occasional warning of 'be careful' or 'not so rough'—most likely for their mother's benefit. More so though, their dad had simply done his best to get through the paperwork part of the ranch business while his sons created havoc around him.

Funny, in all the time since they'd buried their father, the familiar scent of their father's aftershave seemed to still linger in the air. Or perhaps it was nothing more than memories and wishful thinking.

"Did Mom tell anyone why we're all here?" Carson uncapped the crystal decanter behind the desk then raised an empty glass to his brother.

"No thanks." He waved off the silent invitation. "Rachel is unpacking. Neither of us has any idea what this is all about."

Carson sank heavily in one of the oversized leather chairs, swirled the ice in the two fingers of bourbon, and took a long swallow.

"Looks like you've had a hard day." Preston took a seat across from him, leaving the sofa and a smaller chair for his mom and siblings.

"Hard week." Carson eyed the glass glimmering from the reflection of the nearby lamp. "Heck, more like weeks."

Preston leaned forward and threaded his hands in front of him. "What's wrong?"

"Just another day in the flip world. Turns out the most recent project we sank all our available cash into is now knee deep in litigation."

"That's something new."

"For me it is. Seems all the houses in that subdivision are in a class action suit against the original developers and we can't do squat until it's settled. My ninety day rehab schedule just went down the drain."

"So now what?"

"Not sure. I'm okay for a while, but the reno budget is growing tighter every day until I come up with a plan B."

"Sorry, man." Preston changed his mind about that drink after all.

The loose board by the threshold squeaked announcing his sister's arrival. "A little early to be drinking isn't it?"

"What's that saying, it's five o'clock somewhere?" Carson leaned forward and set his drink on the table then looked at his watch. "It's been five on the east coast for over half an hour."

"In that case," Rachel smiled up at Preston still at the bar, "make mine on the rocks."

"Aren't you too young to drink?" Carson teased.

"I should be twenty one again."

"Twenty one? Aren't you sixteen?"

"Here we go again." Rachel accepted her glass and rolled her eyes at her brothers.

Didn't matter how old she grew, in their eyes she and Jillian would always be the kid sisters who needed their big bad brothers to take care of them.

"Never mind that." Preston figured the least he could do was reel in his brother's sense of humor, especially since they had more pressing matters at hand. Setting his drink aside he slid his phone from his pocket and hit his mom's number.

"Mom?" Rachel asked.

Preston nodded, and Carson scooted to the edge of his seat, carefully watching the phone, then sliding back when the call went to voice mail.

"Anyone else starting to feel guilty for making Mom worry when we missed curfew and forgot our phones?"

"Not me," Preston smiled. "I was perfect."

Rachel rolled her eyes at him and then her face stiffened. "Seriously maybe we should make some phone calls. Friends, Ray, make sure she's all right."

"She's a grown woman who has worked this ranch for longer than any of us have been alive,b and running it just fine without Dad. I'm sure she'll be here any minute and laugh off our concerns." Carson's words painted a picture of a calm unconcerned son, but the look in his gaze and leaving a half full drink unfinished spoke volumes to just how concerned he was about their mother's tardiness. What in heaven's name could she be up to?

"Loud noise reactivity. Perceived confrontation. German Shepherd. What time?" Sarah Conroy tapped the pad she'd used to scribble data on the most recent dog needing to be homed. With the sudden onslaught of military working dogs coming through the system her usual sources for fosters were growing slim. There had to be an answer and she'd better find it before Tuesday morning at zero nine hundred hours. A few more details and requisite polite exchange of weather, family, and allergy season, and she disconnected the call and brought her laptop screen to life.

"I have to run." Her father grabbed a protein bar off the counter and shoved it in his jacket pocket, then casually pilfered one, then two, of the chocolate chip cookies she'd made earlier in the day. "Mary Mahoney has finally gone into labor for real."

"Finally?" She'd been daughter to a country doctor long enough, and spent enough summers playing receptionist and aid to know almost as much about medicine as her father. Though every med school in the world would probably disagree with her. Still, even she knew that every pregnant woman eventually finally had a baby.

"She's ten days overdue and every time Braxton hicks start she'd be in my office convinced this was *the* time."

"How do you know this isn't another false alarm?" As sure as she knew her name was Sarah Sue Conroy, she knew there would be a definitive answer.

"Heard it in her voice."

And *that* was why her dad was so very good at what he did. She still remembered the time that Mrs. Harper had called to tell the doc that she was having strong twinges and was going to climb into the tub to relax before the main event. When her husband called back an hour later in a panic, her father told him to hold the phone close to his wife's face so Sarah's father could listen. A few long moments later and the well-loved old doctor informed Mr. Harper not to wait for him, but rather to take his wife to the hospital and don't worry about the speed limits, the sheriff would understand. An hour later Faith Harper was born.

Her father paused long enough to kiss her on the temple. "It's nice to have you back. Not much about the chaos in today's world I'm happy about, but having you working from the house is a welcome change. Love you."

"Love you too. And it's nice to be back." In the half a dozen years since she'd moved to Austin, she hadn't realized just how much she missed living in a sleepy small town. Apparently she missed it all a lot. A whole lot of lot. Especially chatting over dinner about anything from Mildred McEntire's latest bedazzled outfit, to who'd won that day's corn hole match at the park, to the latest fight at the town council over their beloved town of Honeysuckle, Texas. Nary a week went by when there wasn't a disagreement of some kind between the faction who wanted to promote the honeysuckle arts and crafts that filled the Main Street shops with everything from candles to potpourri, and the faction who felt being corn hole capital of Texas was the bigger advantage for promotion dollars.

"Odds are I'll be home late." Her dad stood at the open front door. "First babies usually take their sweet time. If I am, you go ahead and take your mother's casserole out of the oven and invite yourself over to the Sweets. Alice would probably enjoy the company. Even though it's been over a year, she's still a bit out of sorts over losing Charlie, not that she realizes it." He pressed his lips into a thin line and shook his head with a sigh. "Anyhow, company would do her good."

"Will do!"

The front door closed in the distance and Sarah pushed to her feet. A casserole dinner with Ms Alice would be way more fun than eating alone, waiting for her parents to come home. When the women in town got together for whatever planning committee, it always went long, always included some of Abigail Fine's honeysuckle wine, and Sarah's mom always was the last to leave. Hence the stack of emergency casseroles stashed in the extra freezer. Besides, she hadn't seen any of the Sweets since Charlie's funeral. It was a miserable reason to come home and she'd barely had any chance to say more than "I'm sorry for your loss" to the kids she'd lived next door to for most of her life.

According to the oven clock, dinner would be ready in thirty minutes. Enough time for her to get a little work done. Alice had done such a great job with her son's dog, maybe she would have a few suggestions for Sarah. She'd opened a new browser and watched the swirly thing spin when another thought smacked her upside the head. Why not ask Ms. Alice? After all, if she was left alone to rattle around in the big house, a new dog could be just the ticket. That is if Brady and the foster could share Alice and the house. It was the perfect solution really. Therapeutic companionship for everyone. Yes. The more she thought about it the more she was sure this would be the answers she needed. Now all she had to do was convince Alice Sweet.

Sweet Beginnings is available

MEET CHRIS

USA TODAY Bestselling Author of dozens of contemporary novels, including the award winning Aloha Series, Chris Keniston lives in suburban Dallas with her husband, two human children, and two canine children. Though she loves her puppies equally, she admits being especially attached to her German Shepherd rescue. After all, even dogs deserve a happily ever after.

More on Chris and all her books can be found at
www.chriskeniston.com

Follow Chris' Monday Blog at her website
ChrisKenistonAuthor

Follow Chris on Facebook at
ChrisKenistonAuthor

Never miss a New Release!
Sign up for News from Chris:
www.chriskeniston.com/newsletter.html

Questions? Comments?
I would love to hear from you! You can reach me at:
chris@chriskeniston.com

www.ingramcontent.com/pod-product-compliance
Lightning Source LLC
Chambersburg PA
CBHW061547310726
48972CB00008B/2650